CLARA, DREAMING

A FUTURISTIC ROMANCE RETELLING OF THE SANDMAN

A.W. CROSS

Clara, Dreaming

Copyright © 2019 by Glory Box Press

Published by Glory Box Press
British Columbia, Canada.
gloryboxpress@gmail.com

All rights reserved. This book or any portion thereof may not be reproduced or used in any manner whatsoever without the express written permission of the publisher except for the use of brief quotations in a book review. For information regarding permission, write to Glory Box Press at gloryboxpress@gmail.com

First edition, 2019

ISBN 978-1-9995711-3-9

Cover design by Danielle Fine
Interior design and formatting by Glory Box Press
Editing by Danielle Fine

This is a work of fiction. Names, characters, businesses, places, events, and incidents are either the products of the author's imagination or used in a fictitious manner. Any resemblance to actual persons, living or dead, or actual events is purely coincidental.

FOR H, MAY ALL YOUR
DREAMS COME TRUE.

CLARA,
DREAMING

ONE

There he was, sitting on the bench just as they'd arranged. The back of his hair looked freshly cropped, the skin underneath pale against his tanned neck. A thrill of delight shot through Clara. *Did he do that just for me?* That had to be a good sign, right?

The multi-storied Portfade Botanical Conservatory was their favorite meeting place, the humid, almost sultry air clean of salt, unlike the ocean air permeating the city. Birds called overheard, darting in and out of the teeming life of towering succulents and glossy-leafed ferns. The maze of plant beds gave the illusion that their seclusion was complete. Perfect.

She glanced up at the conservatory clock, a garishly oversized, modern rectangular face incongruous with the riot of vines surrounding it. It was so easy to lose track of time here, among the quiet sighing of leaves explored by velvet-winged butterflies.

He may have been on time, but she was two minutes late. Well, *he* would think that, anyway. In truth, she'd been here for over an hour, too anxious to stay home and wait. She'd walked the warren of paths twice to kill time, taking care to keep out of sight of this particular bench, just in case he'd had the same idea. He hadn't. He'd shown up just as the minute hand hit its mark. Did *that* mean anything? He looked cool and calm, while sweat gathered under her armpits, staining the satin of her dress.

Why didn't I wear something sleeveless? She tugged at the fabric, trying to make the dark patch less visible. *Because blue is his favorite color and you couldn't afford to buy a new dress because you spent all your money buying him this.*

Her fingers tightened around the box she clutched. Inside was a heavy gold and hematite watch, thick-cut in a masculine style and engraved with his name. *To Jason, all my love.* She'd even had it imbued with the perfume she wore so he'd be reminded of her constantly. Maybe such a gift was premature, but this time, she'd decided to be bold. Every time before, she'd hesitated, and things had gone wrong. But this time she would nail it. And then…

Go now, before you lose your nerve.

Squaring her shoulders, Clara strode up to the bench and cleared her throat.

Jason turned, and her heart squeezed painfully in her chest as the numbers on the clock and the trilling of the birds faded away. He was so handsome, his dark hair falling carelessly over his cobalt-blue eyes, his crooked smile widening as he saw her. How could the face she'd seen nearly every day of her life always strike her like it was the first time, the lightning bolt of love at first sight?

As he stood to greet her, her nerves rippled white-hot. She couldn't do this. Not again. What if it ended like all the other times? When his look of friendly affection turned to shock then horror then embarrassment, his eyes shifting back and forth as he searched desperately for a way out, for an escape from her.

And her *feelings*.

She'd said it a million times, in a million different ways. And each time, he'd looked at her in some way she couldn't bear. Pity. Amusement. That awkward moment as his mind raced to find some way to let her down easily, to preserve the tatters of the friendship that had sustained them both for so long. And the anger. *Why did you have to ruin it?* his eyes accused her. *Why couldn't you just keep silent and love me from afar? Why did you have to be so selfish?*

Her throat clamped shut, refusing to let air into her lungs. She was going to suffocate right here in front of him, or maybe her heart would explode. Either way, he would be rid of her, spared the inconvenience of letting her down.

I'm sorry, but I just don't feel the same way. Look, I love you too, but as a friend, nothing more. I just don't feel that way about you. I'm not attracted to you like that. There's someone else… How many ways could he say it? How many different cruelties could he subject her heart to?

No. She wasn't ready. She just needed a bit more time. A nicer dress. A better gift, maybe. A more intimate place? Somewhere cooler. Yes. Then things would fall into place. Just a quick change of plans and she would be ready. She was sure of it. Already, confidence flowed through her. Next time, it would be perfect. *She* would be different. And he…he would be too. He would look at her, his eyes shining with love rather than sympathy, and he would drop to his knees in joy and hold out his arms to her…

Clara yanked the visor off her head, careless of the fragile equipment in her irritation. Of all the programs she'd randomly chosen to quality check, it had to be that one. Something that cut too close to the bone for her. What a crappy start to the day.

Warm anger burned behind her eyes at Sienna, the young woman in the simulation. *Just tell him how you feel, for god's sake. Pull yourself together. You're young, smart, attractive. He'd be lucky to be with you. You're the problem. You and your lack of confidence. He says no, you move on.*

So then what's your excuse, Clara? she chided herself. *You're in the exact same position. That's why you're angry.*

Shut up.

"And now you're sitting here arguing with yourself." She picked the visor up from the floor and placed it gently back on her desk. Taking her ire out on her equipment wasn't going to help. The only thing that *would* was the one thing she couldn't do. She gazed down at the profile in front of her.

According to Sienna's file, she'd been running through different versions of this simulation for months, an anxiety therapy exercise that was supposed to help her overcome her fears. Dreaming Life, the company Clara co-owned, had a range of therapy simulations like this, tailored to a patient's specific needs.

It provided a safe space to work through every possible outcome of a scenario in order to give them the confidence they needed in their real lives, to emotionally equip them for whatever happened next. Rejection, loss…it prepared them for all possible negative emotions so they could hold it together if—and when—the worst actually happened.

Why couldn't we program it to go right for a change? Actually give someone the happiness they're seeking?

Because it wouldn't help them. They had to face up to their fears, overcome them. Otherwise, what was the point?

Are you talking about the patients or yourself now, Clara?

For her, even a simulation would be too much. Sienna had more guts than she did, more than she probably ever would. Sienna would overcome her fear one day, but Clara… *I'm doomed to live and die in a pit of unrequited love.*

God, now she sounded like one of Nate's poems. *"Oh, to languish in melancholy…"*

An alert pinged on her interface. Rubbing her eyes, she peered at the screen.

New message from: Nathanael.

Speak of the devil. Clara's chest tightened. Nate. Her Jason. Too eagerly, she hit the keystroke to open it. Was he coming home? Had he finally realized he'd made the wrong decision by going away?

If he does, Clara, you cannot gloat. You know what his pride is like, so swallow yours. The important thing is that he'd be coming home.

She adjusted the projector, and Nate manifested in her office, sitting in the well-worn, cashmere-covered armchair he'd insisted on taking with him from home. He leaned forward, squinted at the recorder, then leaned back and tried to look casual. The illusion was spoiled only seconds later when he leaned forward again, presumably toward his reflection, and ran his hand through his hair. His fingers shook, and a knot formed in the pit of Clara's stomach. Nate never seemed nervous about anything, so what was going on? Was this—

No, it couldn't be.

Hope threw itself against her ribcage, attracted to Nate's image like a magnet.

Could this be the moment she'd been waiting for? Had Nate finally come to his senses and realized he'd loved her all along, not as a sister, but as something more. Was he—

Nate's hologram stared at her, eyes gleaming and face flushed, and Clara's heart sat heavily in her throat, making it hard to breathe. Would he confess straight away? Would it tumble out in a rush, Nate too overcome to waste any more time? Or would he give some sort of convoluted preamble, stretching her to unbearable lengths of suspense before finally catapulting her to the stars? Although he couldn't see her, she smoothed down her own unruly hair and gave a silent prayer of thanks that she wasn't wearing a grubby lab coat.

"Hey, Loth, how's it going? I've..."

The lump in her throat turned bitter. He wasn't going to confess his love for her. He hadn't intended to speak to her at all.

Typical Nate. Too careless to consider the consequences of his actions. But why should he? He didn't know how she felt. She'd always been careful to keep her love close to her chest, tucked away where only she could find it. As far as Nate knew, she was just same old Clara, the girl he'd known all his life, his business partner and betrothed of convenience. He didn't see her. Not the acclaimed scientist, a leader in her field. Not the debutante who'd defied expectations and shrugged off the life of idle indulgence offered to her. And certainly not the curves of the woman instead of the girl.

He didn't see her at all.

TWO

"Lothair." Clara waited impatiently for the sound of her brother's footsteps in the hall. "*Lothair!*" Why didn't she just send the message to him and be done with it? *Because even a scrap of Nate meant for someone else is better than nothing.* It was humiliating.

"For goodness' sake, Clara, I'm right behind you." His hair stuck up in all directions, crowned with the steam rising from the mug he clutched. He wore only a bathrobe—and barely closed at that.

"I was listening out for those ridiculous shoes you wear." She grimaced. "Can you please close that robe, Loth? I can see your—"

"You're awfully prickly this morning, C." He balanced his coffee on a pile of Clara's papers and rearranged his robe, double-knotting it at his waist with a flourish. "Better?"

"*Underwear* would be better." She snatched the mug off her folders and gulped the contents down before Lothair could protest. If her brother insisted on parading around her office half-naked at noon on a weekday, he could damn well share.

The liquid burned a fiery path down her throat, and she doubled over, wheezing. "What the—"

"Lucéat. It *is* after noon, you know." He grinned and threw himself onto the overstuffed couch across from her desk.

"No, it's not. It's 9 a.m." It must be wonderful to be the CEO of a huge corporation. Loth simply paid other people to do everything for him, including his own job. Luckily for them, he was adept at finding just the *right* people.

"I've got a meeting with Arienne in an hour."

Ah. That explained the lucéat. If Clara had to spend a few hours with Arienne, she would've been drinking too. *You're being too hard on him.* In truth, Loth worked every bit as hard as she did, just in a different way. *Smarter, not harder,* as their father would've said.

"What's up, C? You look like *you're* the one meeting good ol' Ari."

She turned her chair toward him, trying to make her expression neutral. "Nate sent you a message. To me. *Again.*" This was the third time. The first had detailed some random sexual conquest he'd made, and the second had been more of the same, only that one had also included some delightful pictures of the lady in question. Clara couldn't bear to see any more. And yet, every time she saw his name as the sender, her stupid hopes rose that maybe, just maybe, her time had come. Completely unaware of her turmoil, Nate's apparition sat immobile, waiting patiently to be brought to life.

Clara had loved Nathanael as long as she could remember. They'd known each other since they were babies, their fathers partners in what would become Dreaming Life, the Blackmoth Republic's premier virtual reality therapy company and the pride of Portfade and Foxwept Province. They'd been unofficially betrothed ever since they were fifteen, a promise made to Clara and Lothair's father on his deathbed. The commitment had been wrung from them as a way to hold their family's empire together, a business arrangement and nothing more, but Clara had meant her agreement with every cell in her body, already knowing at that tender age that she would never love another, not the way she loved Nate.

If only he felt the same. He loved her, of course; of that she had no doubt. But it wasn't the type of love Clara felt for him, and it probably never would be, despite how fervently she wished otherwise. No, when it came to Nate, she had to be happy with whatever crumbs she could get, living in hope that one day he would reciprocate her feelings. Sometimes, she hated herself for it, but she hated the thought of being without him even more. Most of all, she hated herself for not just looking him square in the eye and saying, "Nate, I love you. So do you want to be with me or not?" At least then she could move on with her life either way. But *that* was what she was most afraid of.

The three of them had been joined at the hip most of their lives—until earlier this year when Nate went away to university. Clara had known she'd miss him, but the sheer depth of the void he'd left behind had been unexpected, and she spent many hours gazing out from behind the glass walls of the Dreaming Life ivory tower, trying to will Nate from the Draglight Isles back to her.

Nate, on the other hand, didn't seem to feel the loss. When his father passed away shortly after Nate turned eleven, he'd inherited his father's shares in the company—as well as his seat on the Board of Directors—and subsequently lived his life to the full in the way expected of the young, handsome, and rich.

It broke Clara's heart.

"Well, what's he saying?" Loth stretched out like a cat, knocking Clara's carefully placed throw pillows to the floor.

She ignored the mounting pile of cushions. No matter how many times she rebuked Loth about his lack of respect for other people's things, it fell on deaf ears. "Don't you just want me to forward it to you? It might be private." *You know damn well he'll say no, so why the pretense?*

Loth grinned at his twin. "Nah, we're family. Whatever Nate's got to say, I'm sure he doesn't care if you know."

"I—"

"Just play it, Clara, please. I'm so comfortable." Loth gave her the pleading look she'd never been able to resist. Even when they were children and it meant she would inevitably take the blame for something.

Ugh. Hopefully, it wouldn't be anything too gross. Clara tried to give Nate the benefit of the doubt, but sometimes he pushed it to the limit. *One day, Nate, I'm going to love you a little bit less.* She started the video.

Although his hair was now just the right amount of disheveled, the long black strands escaping his ponytail and framing his face, the rest of Nate didn't look so polished. Purplish smudges shadowed his dark eyes, and his mouth was drawn, like he hadn't laughed or smiled in days. His shirt was rumpled and there were scuff marks on his normally glossy shoes. All in all, he looked very un-Nate-like, and the fear rose in her that there were worse things in the message than yet another beautiful woman.

Nate cleared his throat, as though he knew they were waiting for him to speak. *"Hey, Loth, how's it going? Sorry I haven't messaged you much lately. I've been busy with my studies, you know, the same old crap. Mother's been after me about it, along with Clara. Speaking of which—"* He glanced down at his hands where they twisted in his lap.

At the sound of her name, Clara's pulse quickened. *Oh god.* What if he said something she didn't want to hear? Something she wasn't *supposed* to hear.

He looked back up. *"She's not still dating that idiot Sherwood, is she? Man, that guy's a— Well, I guess I can't blame her. He's good-looking, and with me away…it probably doesn't help that I accidentally sent her those messages. Whoops, haha."* His laugh was brittle. *"Hopefully she didn't take it the wrong way. I mean, Dahlia is great and all, but she's no Clara—"*

"He probably added that last part to cover his ass in case I watched this over your shoulder. Typical." Clara shook her head. Nate was insufferable. *She's no Clara.* So why did the air suddenly feel so thin? And what did he mean by *"with me away?"* What, like she had nothing better to do when he was around than trail after him like a lovesick puppy? Even if it was true at times, screw him. She had her pride. Clara made a mental note to give Sherwood a call that very afternoon. *Maybe I'll accidentally send Nate some choice images of my own.*

"You don't give Nate enough credit, Clar. You're the only one for him."

As always, Loth seemed unaware of the cruelty of his joke. "Then why—"

Loth waved dismissively. "Keep going. I don't want to be late for my meeting, even if it is just Arienne."

Clara made a face at her brother and turned back to the hologram. *"Anyway, I'm not sending this just to say hi. Something happened this week, and I need your advice. It's really shaken me up, and I don't know what to do."*

That was surprising. It wasn't like Nate to be so straightforward about asking for help from anyone, even Loth. And to admit that something was bothering him…it was so out of character. For as long as Clara could remember, nothing had seemed to trouble him. Yes, he could be intense at times, but he was one of those people who seemed to live in the moment, taking life as it came.

Even Loth sat up and paid attention. "Is he okay?" He squinted at Nate's image, as though seeing it for the first time.

"I'm not sure." It was probably something ridiculous, like he'd booked two girls for the same night. But Clara couldn't shake the feeling that there really *was* something wrong.

Nate pulled himself up to sit cross-legged and leaned forward intimately, and Clara did the same. *"You're probably going to laugh at me, but I just can't seem to get over it, Loth. It's weird."* He cracked his knuckles. *"I'll start from the beginning. The other night, someone knocked on my dormitory door, so I opened it. Siegmund was supposed to be coming by with—"*

Well, if it had anything to do with Siegmund, Clara *definitely* didn't want to know. If Nate lived life to the full, Sieg lived it to overflowing. Still, she couldn't bear to leave the room. After all, how often did she get to witness a private conversation between Nate and Loth? Although the three of them had few secrets, there *must* be things Nate only ever shared with her brother. *And now you're missing your chance.* She forced to herself to focus on Nate's image again.

"*It wasn't Sieg, but an optics salesman. You know, the ones who come around with all those lenses and visors that connect you directly to the network or have those crappy, preinstalled virtual reality programs on them. I didn't pay him much attention at first, but then I saw his face and I'm ashamed to say I nearly vomited...*"

Loth frowned. "That doesn't sound like Nate."

No, it didn't. Was the stress of being away from home wearing Nate down? Usually, getting him to be serious about *anything* was a full-time job. Clara's self-pity was swallowed by a growing sense of unease. Something was definitely wrong.

"*You're going to think I'm crazy, or at the very least a fool, but I recognized the man from when I was a kid. I know that may not seem like a big deal, but let me tell you the whole story. I'm hoping you're going to tell me what an idiot I'm being—even now I can picture Clara rolling those gorgeous eyes of hers—*"

"He's got you there, C."

Clara ignored him, though her eyes practically ached to comply.

Nate continued. "*You remember when Dreaming Life was only a few years old and our fathers used to work such long hours? Even on the rare nights I did get to see him for more than a few hours, he began having this visitor. We knew when this guy was coming, because instead of Father reading to us as he normally did, he would pace in his study, smoking those disgusting cigars they used to get sent from Noskos.*"

Clara wrinkled her nose. She remembered those cigars well—and hated them, the sickly sweet smell of overripe fruit overlaid with an ashiness that made the back of her throat itch. Her mother had finally banned them in the house.

"On those days, Mother would rush us to our wing immediately after supper. I was about six at the time, and of course, demanded to know why. And she told us that the Sandman was coming."

Clara paused the recording and glanced at her brother. "Loth? Does that sound familiar to you at all?"

Loth was twisting a loose string from his bathrobe and looking utterly bored. "Nope."

"When I asked her who the Sandman was, she backtracked and said that she'd only meant we were all looking tired, like someone had put sand in our eyes. But even at six, I knew this wasn't true. She'd just spent ten minutes scolding me for making too much noise. I suspected she was only saying that so we wouldn't be scared."

"I think this message is more involved than his academic papers. If he fails this semester, we'll know why." Loth conjured up his transcomm—from where, Clara didn't even want to guess—and typed a quick message. "I'm going to push back my meeting with Arienne. Whatever Nat's rambling about, it's still much more exciting than anything she would have to say." He stared at Clara expectantly. "Well? Go on."

She pressed play.

"So, of course, I asked Bunty—"

Clara groaned. Bunty was Nate and his sister's former governess. She was a lovely woman but had an uncomfortably overactive imagination. She still lived with Nate's mother as a helper, and Clara had to bite her lip at the old woman's fantastical tales every time their families got together. She'd once scared Nate's sister so badly she hadn't sleep for a week and had to be sedated.

"*—and she told me the Sandman visited kids who wouldn't go to sleep and threw handfuls of sand into their eyes, then, when the children crawled out of bed, bleeding and blinded, he scooped them up and took them to his home on the moon, where he dumped them into his nest so that his babies could eat the eyes right out of the naughty children's skulls.*" Nate rubbed his hands down his face.

Clara paused the recording again. "Seriously, Loth, what the hell is wrong with that Bunty?" If Clara's six-year-old self had been told such a thing, she would've kicked Bunty in the shins. Even as a child, Clara had had no time for nonsense.

Loth chuckled. He adored Bunty. "Ah, she's harmless. We used to love that sort of stuff when we were kids. She told us this story one time—"

"Whatever. Let's just finish watching the message." Unlike Nate, Clara had other things to do today, and when Loth got started reminiscing…well, one man caught up in his own ramblings was about as much as her patience could handle today.

"*My mother was annoyed with Bunty, because I immediately connected this Sandman with my father's late-night visitor, and every time I heard his footsteps in the hall as he and my father passed through on their way to his lab, I became hysterical.*"

Nate, hysterical? Clara couldn't imagine that, not even when he was a child. He'd always seemed so carefree; it was why he and Loth had become best friends. How could she not have known about this?

"*This went on until I was ten. Mom wanted to turn the nursery into a crafting room now that we were growing up, so I moved into a new bedroom that also happened to be close to my father's laboratory. Anyway, I got it into my mind that I was going to find out who this mysterious visitor was and what he and my father were up to—so one day, when the cigars came out and I knew a visit was inevitable, I crept into the lab and hid."* He leaned forward again, his voice dropping to a whisper, as though he were still afraid of being found out.

Nate sneaking around in his father's lab? Now *that* she could imagine. Throughout their childhood, Nate and Loth had constantly been in trouble for going where they shouldn't. Not that Clara had been innocent, of course, but she'd been careful not to get caught.

"Sure enough, the visitor came, and he and my father retreated to the lab. When I was sure they wouldn't be able to see me from my hiding place, I gathered up all my courage and peered out—and nearly wet myself, because I knew exactly who he was."

Loth showed some interest at last and perched on the edge of the couch. "Oh, here comes the good stuff. Who do you think it was?"

"Just be quiet and he'll tell you." As though Nate had heard her, he took a dramatic pause before continuing.

"It was Coppelius, the same old bastard who used to come over for dinner every month. My mother couldn't stand him. And of course, from that moment on, the Sandman and Coppelius became inseparable in my mind. His appearance certainly didn't help. He was large and heavy, his skin a jaundiced yellow with flaming red cheeks, glittering green cat's eyes, a big nose, overhung by even bigger bushy gray eyebrows...in fact, he was entirely gray aside from his face, clothes and all. And he made this

whistling noise between his teeth that used to make my hair stand on end."

Loth snorted. "Sounds like a male version of Arienne. I'm sure *she* frightens small children all the time." He rolled his shoulders and settled back against the couch arm. "I actually remember Nate telling me about this guy before...apparently, he used to torture them at those meals by touching their food with his hairy, disgusting hands. It used to drive Sadie to tears."

Everything drives Sadie to tears. But that's what comes from being a spoiled brat.

The day Sadie moved to the other side of the vast Blackmoth Republic had been a great day for Clara, who couldn't stand Nate's delicate, simpering sister. "I wish I'd known that. I'd have been poking her food with both hands."

"Ah, you're just jealous because she's perfect." If by perfect, Loth meant that she looked like a porcelain doll, was willfully ignorant, and charmingly stupid with laughter that pealed like bells and made Clara want to fill her ears with sand, then yes, she was *perfect.*

"Can I go on?"

"Of course." Loth gestured magnanimously and reclined again.

"My mother hated him, turning from a cheerful, vivacious woman into stone the moment he stepped through the door. Father treated him as an honored guest, and Coppelius made sure to milk that for all it was worth. Fancy dinners, expensive wine, you name it." Nate shook his head in disgust.

"So I was hiding, watching, when my father unlocked a cupboard and pulled out a large case. Coppelius withdrew an object from it and they attached a number of thin wires which led into the

port of a tiny computer. It was when they stepped back to admire their handiwork that I screamed.

"Part of it was my father's face, which had transformed from the kindly, gentle one I knew into something ugly—a mirror of that awful man's. The other part was the contents of that case and what they were doing to it. Even now, it fills me with terror." He wiped his palms on his thighs and shuddered.

Loth was balanced on the edge of the couch again, his hand over his mouth. His horrified expression was almost comical. Clara had never seen either of the two men so serious about anything. She shook her head in amusement. This day was turning out to be incredibly bizarre.

"The case was full of eyes. Eyeballs of every color, some in pairs, some alone in their little nest. And the item they'd hooked to the computer? Another eyeball. I don't know what they were doing to it, but the iris convulsed wildly around the pupil while Coppelius just stood there with this crazy grin on his face."

Okay, that *was* pretty appalling. Why had Nate never told them this story before?

"As soon as they knew I was there, Coppelius was on me. He dragged me kicking and screaming out of my hiding place and pinned me to the workstation. He tore the wires from the eye on the table and advanced on me, thrusting the needle-ends of the wires into my face. 'Now we've got eyes—a beautiful pair of children's eyes.'" Nate mimed jabbing the wires into an invisible face, his mouth contorted in a sneer, before glancing back up at his audience.

"My father grabbed him by the arm and pulled him away, begging him to leave me alone, to let me keep my eyes. At first Coppelius resisted, but then he

laughed and...I don't remember much of what happened next." Nate's gazed became fixed somewhere over their heads *"They tell me I had a seizure of some kind. All I remember is pain, excruciating pain all through my body as though my nervous system was on fire. The next thing I knew, my mother was bending over me, kissing me, and telling me I was going to be okay."*

His brow creased. *"Apparently, I'd been out of it for several weeks, and they hadn't been sure I would recover—"* He stopped and shook his head.

"I think I remember when that happened," Loth said slowly. "Don't you? He wasn't able to come to our birthday party that year. His mother said he had some kind of fever."

Clara *did* remember. She'd taken particular care choosing her birthday dress, something frillier than she normally liked; Nate always seemed drawn to that sort of ridiculous, ribbon-covered nonsense. Devastated when her mother told her Nate wasn't coming, she'd gone to bed early, claiming a stomachache from too much cake.

"The first thing I asked my mother when I woke up was whether or not Coppelius was still there, only I called him the Sandman." He grinned wryly. *"She assured me that he was long gone, had left the city the night after my seizure. Obviously, I recovered, but it was during the time I slept that I became color-blind—something which the doctors haven't been able to explain to this day. I also stopped dreaming. Ironic, when you consider our empire."* He took a deep breath and leaned back, his shoulders straight, as though the tension in him had eased.

"So now you know what's been on my mind, Loth. I would've told you sooner, but it sounds

crazy, doesn't it?" Nate's holographic eyes pleaded to the contrary.

It *did* sound crazy. But Nate wasn't the type for melodrama. Whether it had happened like that or not, something had obviously made a significant impact on him.

"So he never—" But as she turned to her brother, Nate spoke again. His face was haunted, deep lines around his mouth aging him prematurely.

"And now I'm going to tell you something I've never told anyone. You can tell Clara, if you like, but only her.

"I'm going to tell you about my father's murder."

THREE

"*Murder?* Since when was Nate's father murdered?" As far as Clara knew, Nate's father's death was a freak accident. There'd been a shroud of secrecy around it at the time, but she'd assumed it was merely their parents trying to protect them.

"I—" For once, Loth was speechless as he reached over Clara's shoulder and paused the recording, his expression hurt. "Why didn't he ever tell me? I thought we told each other everything." He looked for all the world like the eleven-year-old boy who'd woken his sister in the middle of the night so they could creep downstairs and eavesdrop on their mother, who'd gasped into her transcomm then shouted for their father. There'd been a flurry of activity after that, a blur now in Clara's older mind.

"Don't take it personally, Loth. This is the first I've *ever* heard of it too. Maybe he doesn't mean it literally."

Loth nodded, but he looked unconvinced as he restarted Nate's message.

Nate stared down at his fingers. "*It happened a year after the incident in the lab. We were sitting around the table, having supper, when my father's transcomm went off. The minute he looked at the screen, his face went pale and he dropped his fork. My mother guessed right away who it was.*"

Coppelius. She began to cry, and that frightened me more than my own bad memories of him. My father swore to her it would be the last time."

Nate's hand crept up to his throat. *"I couldn't breathe. My mother must've seen my face and worried that I would have another seizure, so she rushed us off to bed before he arrived. That night, I tossed and turned, unable to fall asleep. I must have at some point, though, because I was shocked awake by an explosion so strong it shook the entire house, like that time Loth and I let off those fireworks in the library."* He grinned a little at that before the corner of his mouth fell again.

"I leaped out of bed and ran to my father's lab. Smoke was billowing out the door, a toxic, stinging haze that seared my throat. There was a wild scream, and I rushed in to find my mother collapsed on the floor next to my father's body."

Nate covered his face with his hands and spoke through his fingers. *"His...oh my god, his face, Loth. It was scorched black and distorted, as though he'd died in agony. They told us later there'd been an accident, though they could never explain exactly what had happened. But I knew. Coppelius killed him. My father was trying to sever ties with him and whatever it was they were doing, so he murdered him."* He dropped his hands back down to his lap.

"And before Clara asks, no, I don't have any proof. But Coppelius disappeared from Portfade that night without a trace and has evaded the authorities ever since. Less than an hour later, I got sick like I had before, and recovered only just in time to go to my father's funeral a few days later."

"I remember that day," Loth said slowly. "His father looked so peaceful, so...normal. I never would've guessed—"

Clara's mind raced. Was Nate doing drugs? He and Loth liked a drink, or several, but she'd never know him to take narcotics. But what else could explain…whatever this was?

"So now that I've told you all that, you'll understand why I'm in such a state. That optics seller is him. Coppelius. I know it is. He has a different name—Gordon Vandran—and he looks and dresses differently, but I know it's him. I'd never forget that man and now here he is again, darkening my doorway. I can't help but be afraid of what this means, Loth. I feel doomed. Why would he return after all this time? Why did he want me to see him?

"I have to ask myself, Loth, what does he want from me?"

"He probably wants you to buy his damn optics." Clara pushed her chair back from the desk, irritation pricking at her.

If it wasn't drugs, it must be stress. Nate never should've gone away to Draglight for university. There was a perfectly good one here in Portfade, but he'd insisted on going to the best. What did it matter? He'd always have his shares and his seat on the board. It wasn't like he actually needed to get involved in the day-to-day running of the business. He'd wanted to be an artist when they were growing up and had even begun designing dreamscapes for the company. Then last year, out of nowhere, he'd decided he wanted to get involved in the business side. *A terrible idea from the start.*

Loth looked startled. "What do you mean?"

"Oh please, Loth. You can't be buying this. Either Nate's on drugs or having a nervous breakdown." Something else dawned on her. "Or is this some sort of elaborate prank from the two of you? Because if so, it isn't funny. I wasted the last hour on it when I could've been working." She glanced pointedly at the stack of files on her desk. Unlike Loth, she worked almost exclusively in research and design, testing new theories and experimental products for the company. It wasn't the career she'd originally planned for herself, but she couldn't snub her parents' legacy, and over the years, she'd come to love her work.

Loth held up his hands in surrender. "Clara, I swear, it's not a joke. And I'd know if he was on drugs."

Sometimes Loth didn't seem to know his ass from his elbow, but in this case, Clara believed him. "Fine. Then what about a mental breakdown?"

"I don't think so, C. Have you ever known him to stress over anything?"

"No, but—"

"So maybe what he's saying is *true*. Or at the very least, he believes it is. Which is good enough for me." Loth stood, and Clara didn't have the heart to tell him his robe had fallen open again.

"But it's *insane*, Loth. All of it. If his father's death had been anything but an accident, we'd know about it." Clara shook her head. There was no way Edward had been murdered. "No, I think the pressure of being away from home, going to that stupid university on that stupid island is getting to him."

Loth put a hand on her shoulder. "I miss him too."

Clara turned away. "What are you going to say to him?"

"I'm not sure." Loth shrugged. "But I can't worry about it now—I have that tiresome Arienne to deal with."

"But—"

"I'll get to it later, I promise." He dismissed her with a wave over his shoulder as he sauntered out the door.

Loth was infuriating. But it was so typical of him, all caught up in the drama one minute then completely indifferent the next. It was one of many things that made Clara want to throttle her twin. Well, fine. If he wasn't going to sort this out with Nate, she would. Besides, it was better that way. Left to his own devices, Loth would probably egg Nate on, encouraging this absurdity. No. She was going to nip it in the bud now, before it got out of hand.

FOUR

The moment Nate started the recording, Clara's hologram convulsed into existence, her chin raised in disapproval. She spoke without preamble.

"So, you sent your last message for Loth to me by mistake. Again. I'm starting to think you do it on purpose, maybe because you're too lazy to write us separately? Anyway, we watched it together. He's promised to get back to you later, after his meetings are finished for the day."

Nate paused the hologram. Crap. He'd truly meant to send that last message to Loth. But maybe it *wasn't* an accident, like Clara said. Maybe, on some subconscious level, he'd wanted to send it to her instead of her brother. She was a lot more pragmatic about these things than he was, and that was what Nate needed right now—someone to tell him he was overreacting.

And who better than Clara? He spent most of his time thinking about her. *Clara.* He studied her image. She always wore her dark, curly hair loose and natural, but she'd recently cut it to fall just above her shoulders. It was certainly more sophisticated than when it was longer, more fitting for the woman she'd become. When they were children, he and Loth had delighted in sticking random bits of paper and

26

baubles into her curls and waiting with barely suppressed glee until their handiwork was discovered and Clara dashed after them, shrieking like a banshee.

I wish I could tangle my fingers in it right now.

What he would give for it to be her sitting there with him, rather than just her hologram.

He'd known her all his life, and yet every time he saw her, he was filled with wonder. From the time they were children, he'd known she was the one for him. But over the years, instead of growing closer, they'd seemed to get further apart.

Are you really that surprised?

They couldn't have been more different. She was so damn smart. So serious. And he was so…not. He wasn't stupid, not at all. But his strengths lay in the arts, not in science or business, an oddity in their family's dynasty. Whenever he'd mentioned this to Clara, she'd dismissed it with a wave of her hand, and a derisive, "Don't be ridiculous, Nate." But she was only supporting him like she always did, nothing more. She was surrounded by the brightest Foxwept Province and beyond had to offer every day. How could he compete with that?

He *had* tried—god, how he'd tried—using every weapon in his arsenal to compete, to get her to look his way. But Clara wasn't like other women. She didn't respond to jealousy, his looks, or his fortune. The only thing Nate had ever done that seemed to move her was the dreamscapes he'd created for Dreaming Life. Vibrant and painstakingly detailed, they were woven from his love for Clara into elaborate tapestries that formed the backdrop for treating the ill and dying. Subtle love letters to her that bared his heart and soul.

And yet she hadn't understood.

Or maybe she does, but she's just trying to spare your feelings.

She'd raved about them, of course, but about their therapeutic value, not about how they spoke to her. The failure was obviously his. Well, fine. If what he was now wasn't enough for her, he would change, even if he had to let go of himself in the process.

But it was a challenge. Aside from his talent, she saw him as frivolous and shallow. And why shouldn't she? The parties, the booze, the women...especially the women, anything to try lessening his painful awareness of her and his unrequited love. He'd made so many mistakes. Sometimes he was surprised Clara still spoke to him.

He'd been keenly aware of his inadequacy ever since their betrothal. She probably didn't take it seriously—hell, she probably didn't even remember it—but he did. He'd clung to it every day since her father died, determined to become the man her father had thought he'd be—the best choice for his daughter and not, like the small voice inside him whispered, the best choice for the business. Perhaps the worst part was that Clara might go through with it for that reason alone; she was so much like her father that way.

But that was the last thing he wanted. He wanted her to marry him because he was the right man for her. The man she *wanted*. So he would become a businessman, qualified to lead alongside her and Loth, not just an heir to an empire. Then Clara would finally look at him the way he'd always dreamed—as something more than an old friend.

And even though he had a long way to go, he had hope. Hope that he could still win Clara over. Take this message, for example. Here she was in his hour of need. She wouldn't do that if she didn't truly care for him, right? And against all caution, the old hope rose in him that maybe things between them could still work out. He poured a stiff drink and settled himself before restarting the recording with a shaking finger.

Clara's image raised a haughty eyebrow. "*Seeing as you and Loth keep teasing me about my 'cool-headed temperament,' I'll give you the benefit of it now.*"

Nate smiled despite himself. He and Loth had made fun of her seriousness all their lives. They often joked that if the tower was burning to the ground, Clara would stop and make sure the papers on her desk were organized before she fled.

"*I admit, when I first heard your message, I was upset. What you told us...Nate, I'm so sorry. We never really knew what happened to your father—you know how secretive our parents were—and I feel terrible that you've carried it with you all this time.*" She raised her hand to cover her heart, and Nate's throbbed in response. Finally telling them the dark secret he'd carried for so long had lifted a massive weight from his shoulders, and yet, it was as though a ghost had settled in its place. Maybe, with Clara's help, he could banish that burden forever.

He'd never wanted Clara and Loth to know he'd kept it from them. They'd made a promise, the three of them, when they were children, to tell each other everything. It had seemed like the most solid bond in the world then. He wrapped his shaking fingers tighter around his glass and kept listening.

She let out a long sigh and her gaze searched the ceiling. "*But, Nate, the other stuff...this optics dealer, Coppelius. I think—and please,*" she looked straight ahead, as though right through him, "*don't be angry with me—that maybe you're not taking care of yourself as well as you could be. There's no shame in it, Nate. University is incredibly stressful and being a reluctant partner in one of the most prestigious medical technology companies in the Blackmoth Republic in your mid-twenties is a lot of pressure, especially with your temperament."*

Reluctant partner. Especially with your temperament. The glass shattered in his hand. Clara thought he was buckling under the pressure, that he wasn't cut out for something as serious as business. That was exactly what he *hadn't* wanted her to think. He wiped the blood welling from his palm on his pants. Damn. Maybe he should've watched his message before he sent it. He'd tried to convey it as calmly as he could—and he'd clearly failed. And now Clara thought even less of him.

But she wasn't done humiliating him. *"I'm not trying to dismiss what you said, not at all. I'm just trying to give you some perspective in the cold light of day. Here's what I think happened."*

She didn't believe him. She thought he was being ridiculous, as always. But he knew what he'd seen. *Who* he'd seen. All the reasoning in the world couldn't change that. And if it had been anyone else...but Clara could say things to him that no one else, not even Loth, could. He would humor her and hear her out. Maybe she *could* change his mind.

I would give anything if she can.

"I think this Coppelius made a big impression on you when you were a child. And why wouldn't he? You've always been sensitive, and he obviously hated children. Combine that with the late-night visits and secretive work your father and he did...it's no surprise your child's mind made him a bogeyman, of sorts. And I'm sure Bunty did nothing to dissuade

you of that." Her eyes rolled to the heavens and Nate snorted.

If only Clara knew that Bunty often went out of her way to provoke her. At their last family dinner before Nate went away, Bunty had told them a fantastical tale about a person she knew who lived in the wilds beyond the Perimeter in a house that sat upon the legs of mutated animal bones and *breathed.* Clara's eye had begun to twitch, and Nate had barely made it out to the balcony before bursting into laughter.

But what Clara had said was true enough. Bunty had always encouraged his and Sadie's imaginations, much to the chagrin of his mother, who'd constantly followed them around, tidying up whatever mess their adventures had left in their wake. She'd been too mortified to get the cleaning woman to do it, worried that the gossip that her children weren't perfect little angels would reach the ears of someone who cared, though Nate couldn't for the life of him imagine who that would be.

"But at the end of the day, your father's work was in the experimental stages then. He used to make the same late-night trips to our house, remember? Those sessions also involved the use of mock eyes and optics. Your mother was probably disturbed about it for the same reasons mine was—they tossed a lot of time and money away on too many different theories instead of just focusing on the one which would eventually define Dreaming Life. Plus, and let's be honest here, our fathers' work meant they were rarely home, and I know that bothered my mother. I'm sure it bothered yours too."

He had to give her that as well. But he'd never felt that way when Clara's father had visited, and neither had his mother. No, Coppelius had been different.

Still, the visceral horror he'd felt the last twenty-four hours was already ebbing as Clara's logic worked its magic.

"Now, about your father's death. I did some digging and, Nate, there were all the right things in your father's lab to cause such an explosion. An accident, a terrible accident, is the most likely explanation." She rushed on, as though she knew how that would make him feel. *"Please, Nate, don't think I'm being cold. Quite the opposite. I know the anniversary of your father's death has just passed, and I'm sure that's having an effect on you, whether you realize it or not."* He had to drop his gaze from the sympathy in her eyes.

Could she be right? He checked the calendar on his transcomm. The seventeenth. Three days after the anniversary of his father's accident. She'd remembered. He hadn't—at least, not consciously.

"I think that this combined with the stress you're under in a perfect storm when that optics dealer knocked on your door, and your mind made a leap it wouldn't have otherwise. Think about it. Why would this Coppelius, a notorious scientist, be working as an optics seller? And even if he were, why track you down all these years later just to knock on your door and try to sell you something?" She folded her hands in her lap, pleased, as though her answer was definitive. *"It doesn't make sense."*

No, it doesn't, and that's why I was so freaked out.

But... His mind groped to recall the twist in his gut at seeing Vandran's face leering from his doorway and couldn't. A meek man with similar green eyes and a nose as prominent as Coppelius's rose instead. Had he been that mistaken? Could Clara be right? Was it all in his mind? He dropped his head into his hands, ignoring the drying blood on his fingers. Maybe she *was* right. She always had been in the past. He *was* under a lot of pressure, though he hated to admit it. He'd always thought of himself as being above all that, cool and unruffled, his destiny assured even if it wasn't necessarily the one he'd chosen. Well, maybe he'd gotten cocky.

Her voice took on a stern, unyielding tone. *"You need to start taking better care of yourself, Nate."* And then she said what he knew she'd been thinking all along. *"Come home. You can learn everything you need to know about running the business on the job. If you were going to be one of our scientists, I agree, university is a must. But not for you. Or—and don't be annoyed—why not just go back to your art? The dreamscapes you were building were incredible. You'd keep your seat on the board, but you'd get to do something more suited to you."*

That she was wrong about. Yes, maybe he did need to start looking after himself more, but he wasn't going to leave university or give up trying to get more involved in Dreaming Life. Not when he was trying to become the kind of man Clara needed.

And she knew his stubbornness well. Her amber eyes narrowed. *"But if you won't do that, then you have to forget this whole matter. Let your father rest. See someone about it. Forget Coppelius. And if you can't do that, and he bothers you again, tell me, and I'll come to Draglight and kick his ass."* She wavered once, and was gone.

Nate dug his fingers into the couch. What must she think of him now? Just when he'd thought she couldn't think worse of him after the Delia—or was it Dahlia?—incident, he'd managed to outdo himself. *Well done, Nate.*

33

Well, he could make it better. He knew when to surrender. He would simply message her back, laugh at himself, and agree that, yes, he probably wasn't taking the best care of himself. He would thank her, admit she was right, and promise to make an appointment with the university counselor. Whether he would actually do it was another matter, but she didn't need to know that.

And when he went home in two weeks, things would change. He would finally be brave and tell her the truth, that she was everything to him, that all the flings he'd had were out of frustration that she didn't seem to take him seriously, to *see* him. That even if he wasn't good enough for her now, he would be. And he would ask her, with no room to hide, if they had a future together, not just as business partners and friends, but as something more. *Everything* more. If she said yes, he was going to get down on one knee and make their childhood betrothal of convenience an official one of love.

He wandered over to his bed and lay down. His mind was easier than it had been since Vandran had knocked on his door, and he was exhausted. He would think now of Clara, of her golden eyes and the smile she kept just for him, less frequent though it might be. Yes, he would hold her in his mind as he went to sleep, and when he woke, the world would be right again.

FIVE

Nate's image appeared in Clara's office once again. He still looked tired, but at least he was smiling.

"*Hi, Clara, how are you? Sorry it took me a few days to get back to you, but I wanted to think over what you said.*" His expression was serious.

What? Nate had actually taken the time to think things over for once? *That* was a pleasant surprise. After she hadn't heard back from him, Clara had worried Nate thought she was dismissing his feelings. Instead, it seemed like he'd listened to her this time. Hm. Maybe he *was* growing up, after all. Could she dare hope? She'd been staring out the window of her hundredth-floor office as usual, her forehead pressed to the cool glass as she'd gazed out at the city of Portfade, thinking about him, about their childhood, and wondering if they were irreparably broken. But maybe not.

He held up his hands. "*First off, I want to apologize for sending that message to you by mistake. I know it wasn't the first time—and the less said about that, the better—and it probably won't be the last.*" A slight blush crept up his neck. "*But you know, I'm glad I sent it to you. I got a lot more sense from you then I would've gotten from Loth—when he bothered to get back to me. He's too used to you doing that sort of stuff for him.*" His voice held no hint of irony.

"*And secondly, I want to say thank you. Everything you said was true. I have been under a lot of pressure trying to study and pay attention to my share of the business at the same time. Maybe I need to be more like Loth and just pay someone else to do both? Then I could spend my days back in Portfade sitting with you in the garden terrace and admiring our kingdom.*" His easy grin made Clara's breath catch in her throat. "*Well, one day, perhaps. In the meantime, I'll take your advice and go speak to someone. I never really dealt with my father's death the way you and Loth did with the death of your parents. You know me, I'm much better at avoiding these sorts of serious things.*" He gave a self-conscious laugh.

This new Nate was a surprise. It wasn't like him to submit so readily. Despite his often-frivolous attitude, he'd had to be strong for his mother and sister for so long, had carried the weight of his father's death, that he often fought even when there was nothing to fight about, especially when it came to someone telling him he was wrong. As for the garden terrace...well, that was another joke. He'd often tease about them settling down and growing old together—right before he'd jet away with Loth to some private island of scantily clad nymphs. So as much as the vision of the two of them might make Clara's heart beat a little faster, she would've been foolish to think it was anything more than an impulsive wish on his part.

"*Something interesting has come of my little flare of insanity, however—I've started to dream again. Strange, right? I have no idea why, but I don't really care. It's so nice...novel, really. And since I know that's your area of expertise, I thought you could analyze mine, see if it tells you anything interesting about people who suddenly start to dream again. I promise, they're not dirty, though I am crossing my fingers that you'll come to me in my dreams one of these nights.*" This time, his smile was mischievous. "*I got some recording equipment from one of the professors here—who was totally fanboying over your research, by the way—and I've attached the results below.*"

He'd started to dream? That *was* strange. Had the run-in with the optic seller unlocked the trauma that had stopped them in the first place? Maybe the experience which had so upset Nate was a good thing after all, a kind of radical therapy.

I can't wait to see what he dreamed about.

It would be the first time she witnessed the dreams of someone who hadn't dreamed for years. And for it to be with someone she knew so intimately…anticipation couldn't even begin to describe the tingling in her chest.

At the very least, it would give her some time with Nate, no matter how vicarious.

"*But—and this will cheer you up—you were totally right. Vandran is not Coppelius. Though I'll be honest, it wasn't just your reasoning that made me see it.*"

There's the rebellious Nate I know. Always having the last word.

"*We have a new business professor at the university, Spalazani, and he happened to overhear me talking to Sieg about Vandran. He told me that the man had been making unsolicited visits all over Draglight, and after a number of complaints, was politely asked to leave town. And he did.*"

"I still stand by my first impression of him, and I feel better now that he's gone, but I'll also admit it was never Coppelius to begin with. Consider the incident over."

But was it? Nate seemed to be acquiescing to all of this just a little too quickly. Where was his natural stubbornness? His resistance on principle alone? Clara had been desperate for Nate to change, to grow up, but now that it seemed to be happening, it didn't feel quite right.

You're just never satisfied, are you?

Nate's hologram continued, unaware of Clara's concern. *"But enough about that! You'd laugh if you met this Spalazani fellow. He's one of the most unusual-looking men I've ever seen. Short and fat, with high cheekbones, beady little eyes, and great protruding lips. He looks like a fish. I expect any minute for him to realize he's left the ocean and fall to the floor, writhing and gasping for breath. A nice man, but I have no idea how he managed to have a daughter as stunning as Olympia."* As he said her name, he dropped his gaze.

And there, right there, was the Nate she knew. That was why he'd managed to get over it so quickly. A beautiful woman. A bitter laugh rose in Clara's throat.

"I saw her the other day for the first time when our class went over to his residence for an after-class chat. Anyway, on my way to the bathroom, I walked past an open door and saw her. He never even told us he had a daughter, though after seeing her, I'm not surprised. He probably thought we'd lose any interest in anything he had to say if we knew she was there—and he's undoubtedly right."

His eyes took on an intense gleam. *"She looks like an angel, Clara, I kid you not. But I also suspect she's a bit of a snob. I waved at her, just trying to be friendly, and she stared right through me, like I wasn't there, standing twenty feet away from her, waving like an idiot. Her face didn't even move. Rumor has it that he keeps her locked up—it's said jokingly, but no one's ever spoken to her. But hey, who needs a personality when you're gorgeous, right?"* He started suddenly, as though he'd just realized who he'd be sending the message to. *"Oh well, forget her. I have."*

No, he damn well hasn't. Clara knew Nate better than he knew himself. This was how it always began. A seemingly offhand observation. A denial. Over-the-top protestations. Then a whirlwind romance that inevitably ended with Nate having to change his contact details, and a broken-hearted woman, her makeup running down her face as she banged on the glass door of the Dreaming Life building, begging to plead her case.

"I'm not sure why I'm telling you all this. Normally, I reserve this sort of stuff for Loth. But I know you don't have a jealous disposition, not over me, anyway, so what's the harm? You're the only one for me, Clara. I'm just waiting for you to realize it. I'm home in two weeks, and I think we should have a talk. About everything."

I don't know why you felt the need to tell me about Olympia, either.

It was perverse quirk of his, telling her he loved her one moment then stabbing her in the heart and twisting the knife the next. It had been this way their entire lives, and yet they just couldn't seem to let each other go. She should confront him, tell him how deeply these flirtations hurt her, and ask him to stop. But she wouldn't. She never did.

"Anyway, speak to you soon, Clara. I miss you. I can't wait to see you. Love you, as always." He flashed her a final grin and disappeared.

You need to tell him how you feel, despite the risk. Then she would know for sure—either he loved her the way she loved him, or...he didn't.

But maybe she wouldn't have to. Maybe that was what he meant when he'd said they needed to talk. That now that he'd gotten away from her out into the big, wide world, he'd realized what she'd feared all along—that he really did see her as nothing but a sister, that there was more to life than her, than the future the child-versions of them had pretended they would have. She'd dreaded that moment for so long, but living in fear of it had become exhausting. She accused Loth and Nate all the time of not taking responsibility for their actions, but she was just as bad.

No. Two weeks from today, she would put her foot down. She transferred his dream data into her immersion system and put on her visor. Maybe there would be something in his dreams that could tell her his true feelings. She sighed as she pulled up the program she'd designed.

Two weeks.

SIX

Clara opened her eyes. She lay on her back in a familiar bed in a familiar room. Nate's room, from when he was a child—a young child, an abundance of brightly painted toys and tiny underpants strewn across the floor. Bunty had been slacking again.

She sat up slowly, trying to keep her movements measured and deliberate. Dreams, even recorded ones, were fragile, flighty things, and until she was sure she was in the throes of it, she had to be careful. So far, so good.

She pulled back the covers, revealing the white organza dress that was her uniform whenever she studied dreams. When Nate had gifted the dress program to her on the day she'd graduated, she hadn't been able to wait to put it on.

Looking at her reflection in the mirror, she'd been taken aback. The color, the demure neckline, and the yards of flowing fabric that billowed behind her as she walked through the dreamscapes—it could've easily been mistaken for a wedding dress. And Nate had given it to her. For a few days afterward, she'd been shy around him, sure that the dress was the start of something. How could it not be? The man she was in love with had given her a dress fit for a bride. But Nate had been oblivious, and it hadn't taken her long to conclude that everything about the

41

dress was a fluke. Her first instinct had been to delete the program, but she hadn't been able to make herself do it. Even if it was a scrap tossed unthinkingly at her, it was a gift from him all the same.

At first, she'd felt faintly ridiculous traipsing around various dreamscapes dressed like a princess on her wedding day, but over time, she'd gotten used to it, and now, it was like her talisman, her anchor, reminding her where she was when the dreams got too intense.

As her feet touched the floor, minuscule sprouts unfurled from the carpeting and the smell of damp earth permeated the room. Faster and faster, they multiplied, until the whole floor was blanketed with tiny green plants. The sprouts grew and flourished blossoming into a wall-to-wall bouquet of every kind and color of flower imaginable. The stems of the blooms stretched and thickened, dropping their petals to the floor as they burgeoned into slender trees with shining emerald leaves.

Sensations flowed through Clara—the sting of a first scraped knee, the thrill of staying up past bedtime, the tears after a fight with a beloved friend. With each new feeling, the forest around her grew denser and darker, forming a canopy overhead until she could see nothing but the trees. The scent of wet soil deepened, overlaid with the stronger smell of something long decayed.

The lush green leaves changed from the gold and orange of autumn to the last gasp of crimson before snowfall. Nate's favorite time of year. Wonder surged through Clara, the pure awe that came from the open mind of a child.

But as the room darkened under the weight of the forest, the red leaves began to fall and Clara understood, beyond a shadow of a doubt, that she must gather every single leaf before it touched the ground. Frantically, she scrambled to catch them, holding her skirts out to receive them before all was lost. Thicker and thicker, they fell; it was an impossible task, one that would suffocate her. She would be buried beneath these leaves, her body to lie undiscovered beneath them until they rotted away.

She couldn't do it. She wasn't good enough, fast enough, smart enough. Leaves drifted down all around her, but her skirts stayed empty. Even as she reached out to pluck one from the air, it slipped through her fingers. Guilt gnawed at her with a chill as bitter as the coming winter. No matter what she did, how hard she tried, she wasn't enough. She was helpless. Incapable. She was...

Back in her office, her breath coming in shallow gasps, her heart pounding a painful rhythm of despair.

Poor Nate. When he'd said he'd started dreaming again, she'd hoped his dreams had been comforting, or adventurous...anything but the misery she'd just witnessed. Clara had seen some pretty cryptic dreams in her time, but this wasn't one of them.

I wonder what Nate will make of it.

She pulled the visor off her head and checked her reflection in the hand mirror in her desk drawer. She looked tired, but that wasn't anything new. Maybe she should call Nate after she'd had a nap and a shower.

He beat her to it.

Her terminal chimed with the special tone she'd reserved for him. Most calls were routed through her secretary, but there were a select few people Clara allowed to contact her directly.

She quickly checked her mirror again, frowning at the face looking back. Should she pretend that her visual system wasn't working? Just let him hear her voice?

No, of course not. Stop being so stupid.

Why should she worry about that? He didn't care how she looked. They'd known each other their entire lives—slightly smoother hair and unshadowed skin wouldn't make a difference now.

Annoyed at both of them, she accepted his call. A second later, Nate's beloved face filled the screen.

He looked as gorgeous as usual. His olive cheeks were ruddy, as though he'd just come in from the fresh air, his black hair perfectly tousled. Damn him.

"Clara! You're looking beautiful as always."

Liar. But she refused to feel self-conscious. She was what she was.

"Hi, Nate. You seem well."

"Why so formal? I hope you're not going to be so stiff when I'm home in a couple of weeks."

"I'm not being—" She bit her lip. Two seconds, and he'd already managed to goad her. "What have you been up to?"

"Not much." He disappeared off-screen briefly, and glass clinked softly in the background. He returned and flopped down in his chair, holding two fingers of amber lucéat in the cut-crystal tumbler she'd given him. Well, allowed him to steal from her office. "Just getting ready for exams."

"Do you *feel* ready?" What she really meant was, *have you actually bothered to study?*

And he knew it. He scowled. "*Yes*, Clara. In fact, Professor Spalazani has been giving me some extra tutoring."

"Spalazani. Is he the new professor you told me about? The one with the stuck-up daughter?" She kept her voice carefully neutral.

"That's the one. Only, I was wrong about Olympia. She isn't stuck up at all. She's just shy. Very cultivated, though. In fact—"

That's what you get for asking. "So I analyzed your dream." The less Clara had to hear about the wonderful Olympia, the better.

"And? Am I nuts?" There was an edge to his voice that gave Clara pause. What was going on with him?

"Yes, but not when you're dreaming. The dream I saw, the one in your bedroom with the leaves, is pretty standard fare."

"Oh." He sounded faintly disappointed. "Really? Because I felt like I was going to suffocate. I woke up in a cold sweat after that one."

"That's just because you haven't been aware of your dreams for so long. For most people, it's a fairly normal dream."

"Normal? It felt quite dark to me."

"Yes, and *that's* normal too. One thing I've learned from studying people's dreams, Nate, is that everyone has both a light and a dark side."

"Even you, Clara? I'll never believe it." He grinned.

She ignored his teasing. "Whenever people feel a darkness inside themselves—like thoughts and feelings they wouldn't normally have—well, it's natural to blame outside factors. But I believe there's no external force, that the darkness is already *within* us, all of us. And yes, even me."

Especially me.

Clara's darkness showed its face to her more often than she would've liked, writhing just below the surface of her skin. Even now, she could feel it, urging her to do something, anything to shock Nate, to make him *see* her. And like always, she swallowed it down.

How could she explain it to him? "That darkness lies dormant until some event triggers it." *Like some tart named Dahlia.* "But it's still *us*, and it only overtakes us if we let it. I'm not talking about real mental illness, Nate, but the more sinister side of ourselves that we all possess."

Nate frowned. "But if that's the case, how do we stop it from taking over?"

"By accepting that it exists without giving in to its impulses. If we can do that, the darkness will be subverted and unable to take hold."

"So you think my dark side was somehow triggered?"

"Absolutely. If you've previously given into it, it leaves a mark which then manifests in unexpected ways. I think it first happened to you when you were a child, during the incident with Coppelius. Your fear of him became a self-fulfilling prophecy, your shadow. But the darkness only succeeds because we think it apart from ourselves and out of our control—the same thing can be said of our lighter sides."

"You sound like a therapist," he grumbled. "Or maybe like that cult on Leandevil."

Clara ignored him. "Accept these dark feelings inside you, Nate. It's your fear of them that gives them power over you and makes them dangerous. Like when Vandran came to your door." She stopped. Had she said too much? Did he think she was patronizing him? It wouldn't be the first time he'd accused her of that.

But if he felt belittled, he didn't show it. "Then what does the dream itself mean?"

"My opinion? It means that feelings you've been suppressing since childhood are finally resurfacing. Given the incident with the optics dealer, I think that's pretty self-explanatory."

"Okay, I can see that. And the leaves? Why did I have to catch them? Why couldn't I?"

"I think that goes back to Coppelius and what happened with your father. You were scared when they caught you, unable to defend yourself. Then, you missed the moment of your father's death, and couldn't do anything to prevent it or to save him." She put her elbows on her desk and leaned her face closer to the screen. "It was probably the first time in your life you felt helpless and incapable, literally watching something happen before your eyes and being unable to stop it. That's where the guilt comes from as well."

"You felt the guilt?" He tossed back a gulp of lucéat and winced.

"Of course. I feel everything when I'm in people's dreams."

"*Everything?*"

"Yes." It had taken some getting used to. People dreamed in ways and about things that didn't even occur to them when they were awake. Often those things were trivial, but sometimes, they were dark and disturbing. It had certainly been an eye-opener for her in terms of people's psyches.

"Even the erotic ones?" He would ask that.

She sighed. "Yes, Nate, even the erotic ones."

"Would you tell me about them? What do they feel like?" He was no longer smiling. He'd leaned closer to the screen as well, his gaze boring into her.

How much had he had to drink? "No, of course not. Patient confidentiality, remember?" Besides, she couldn't express those things to Nate, of all people.

It would be mortifying. And arousing, which was far worse.

He waited for a minute, as though hoping she would reconsider. When she didn't, he slumped back in his chair. "You're no fun, Clara."

"So you and Loth keep telling me. Well, one of us has to be serious, and it certainly won't be either of you."

"Do you really feel that way about me? That I can't take anything seriously?" He avoided looking at her, seemingly fascinated by the liquor as he swirled it in his glass.

She'd only been half-serious and she'd said far worse things to him before, so why had it bothered him this time? He looked practically sullen.

"Nate, are you okay?"

He didn't seem to hear her. It was like he'd forgotten she was even there.

"*Nate.*"

He started then grinned at her. "Sorry, Clara. I'm fine. Just a little tired. All this new dreaming is exhausting."

"Have you had similar dreams since the one you sent me?" If he was dreaming every night about guilt and helplessness, no wonder he wasn't sleeping well.

"I'm not sure. Lately, I haven't been able to remember them. I mean, I know I'm dreaming—I can almost catch wisps of them when I wake up—but I can't remember any more than the odd flash or image." He rubbed the back of his neck. "Is that weird?"

Clara shrugged. "Not really. It's hard to say with dreams. We don't know very much about them—even with all our research. Especially with adults who've only started dreaming. That's why my analysis of your dreams is so important."

"Everything you do is important." He stared at her again with that intense gaze.

What in the world was going on with him? If she hadn't known better, she would've thought he was flirting with her.

In your dreams, Clara.

Hopefully he couldn't see the flush rising in her cheeks. "I'll keep that in mind the next time you and Loth make fun of me for working on a Friday night." She managed what she hoped was a normal smile. "Look, just keep sending me your dreams, okay? I'll let you know if I find anything...strange."

"Thanks, I appreciate it. And Clara," he put his glass down and pressed his fingers to the screen, "I really miss you. I mean it. Life without seeing you every day just isn't the same. I wouldn't wish it on my worst enemy. I love you. In so many ways."

Clara waited for the thrill to rush through her at those words, but it didn't come. There was something sad about them, desperate. Not the way she wanted to hear such a sentiment spoken. Not from him, anyway.

He hurts me in a million different ways and doesn't even realize.

"I love you too, Nate." She kept her tone casual, appropriate for an old friend. "I'll see you in two weeks, okay? We'll talk more then, like you said."

"Okay, Clara. I can't wait." But his face was downcast.

"Nate, are you honestly okay? Do you want me to give you something to help you sleep better? Make your dreams more...pleasant?"

For some reason, it was the wrong thing to say.

"No. Thanks, Clara, but I'm a big boy. I might not be good at much, but I'm sure I can manage *sleeping* on my own. Goodbye." He leaned forward again, and the screen went black.

Clara gaped at the empty screen. What had she said to upset him so badly? There was definitely *something* going on. He obviously wasn't going to tell her, but maybe he would speak to Loth. Her nap and shower could wait. She needed to find her brother and give him two weeks to figure it out.

SEVEN

Nate itched with agitation at the long elevator ride to the top of the Dreaming Life tower. It seemed to be taking forever. He couldn't wait to throw himself into the arms of the people he cared for most in the world. He hadn't even bothered to stop by the complex in the penthouse, where they all had their apartments, for a cleanup.

The two weeks since he'd spoken to Clara had passed in agonizing slowness. And yet, every time he sat down to message or call her, neither the inspiration nor the words would come.

But none of that mattered now. Today, he would see her again, her beloved face and kind eyes, which would ease the tightness in his chest. He would apologize for his tantrum when he'd hung up on her...but how much should he say? Should he declare his true love for her once and for all? He'd tried before in various ways—some subtle, some more obvious—but each time she'd played it off as a joke or a taunt.

If I only knew why, I'd know what to do.

Was it that she saw him as a brother? They *had* grown up together. To him, the familiarity only made his feelings stronger, but was it different for her? Was that why she took his affection for her as playful banter?

Could it be that she, with her painfully practical mind, thought that if their romance went wrong, their friendship would suffer? Or that the business would? That was exactly the kind of harsh reasoning Clara was known for. Acting impulsively was not one of her strengths.

Or maybe she simply didn't think he was good enough. He couldn't blame her for that—he felt it himself. But he was trying to change, and she *knew* that. Still, the pressure of living up to her expectations was exhausting, and fear of her disapproval made the path he was determined to climb all the more slippery.

Or was it his greatest fear: that she simply wasn't attracted to him? If that was the case, he was screwed.

But she hadn't broken off their betrothal. Was that a good sign? Or was it just because she'd promised her father?

If only he knew which way she would go. Childhood Clara would've kept her promise to her father no matter that it *had* been a promise of convenience. But adult Clara was too practical to let a dead man dictate the terms of her life, even if that man was her father. *That* Clara would do what she wanted.

So the question was, did he have the nerve to ask her? There were so many wrong answers and only one right one, as far as he was concerned. Was it better to live in uncertainty but with hope? Or to face up to reality and the possibility of crushed dreams?

Speaking of dreams... He fingered the nanocomm in his pocket. It contained his latest dream plus a patch so that the recordings would be sent straight to her. It was yet another way to forge a link between them, and if her research was the vehicle, so be it.

Perhaps she'd see more of his soul in his dreams and would understand his true feelings without him having to say a word.

But even if he got cold feet about declaring his true feelings today, he had other things to discuss with Clara and Loth. He'd been brooding about the light and dark sides of human nature and had come to some conclusions that were a better fit for his *temperament*, as Clara called it.

It should make her happy, at least, that I've taken her words to heart.

The elevator chimed softly as the doors opened onto the garden terrace, and Nate's pulse quickened. Finally, he would see her in the flesh.

Voices rose from behind the sculpted topiary, not only of his beloved Clara, but also his mother and Lothair. *My entire world.* It was all he could do not to break into a run, to throw himself at their knees and bare everything in his heart.

He shook his head. *You're getting carried away, Nate.* Lothair wouldn't blame him—their tendency to show everything they felt was the same—but the imagined look on Clara's face, the faint disapproval and suspicious lift of her eyebrow were enough to slow his pace to a dignified walk.

He entered the cloistered seating area and stopped. Clara had her back to him, inclining her head in her thoughtful way as Nate's mother spoke. He cleared his throat, and when they turned, their faces open and beaming, he received a profound shock.

Clara was infinitely changed.

Before today, reuniting with her had meant the light becoming brighter, the colors around him more vibrant. His heart would leap in a rhythm that was just for her, and his soul would be soothed with a single glance at her face. Even heaven, if it existed, couldn't compete with her.

But who was this woman? She looked like Clara, but rather than break apart under her brilliance, the heavens merely shrugged and turned away.

Everything about her that had once captivated him was now plain, a face and body he wouldn't look at twice passing in the street. What had happened to her?

She appeared to be thinking the same about him. Her hand seemed to fly to her mouth of its own accord, and her eyes widened in a way he once would've found charming, but which now irritated him.

"Nathanael!" The next thing he knew, Mother had swept him up in her arms, showering his face with kisses. He resisted the urge to push her away, the woman he'd never had an unkind thought about in all his life. Instead, he returned her embrace for as long as he could bear it before gently disentangling himself. The shock of Clara's transformation had pushed all the joy of seeing her again out of his mind.

Beaming, Mother stepped aside and Lothair stood next in line, grappling Nate into his characteristic bear hug and thumping him heartily on the back. "At last, you gorgeous bastard! It's so good to see you." Loth had tried, in his way, to send his own message of comfort to Nate, but as usual, his attempt had been haphazard and lacking any insight. He'd meant well, but their friendship was based on the comfortable and the pleasurable, the careless bond between two brothers who knew beyond a doubt that they would be in each other's lives forever.

Finally, Loth stepped back, and he and Mother made their excuses and left, she to inspect the supper she'd meticulously planned, and Loth to confirm the arrangements he'd made for later that night.

Then it was only Nate and Clara, and the moment he'd wished and waited for so impatiently was now heavy with awkwardness.

"You're as radiant as always, Clara," he lied.

"I wish I could say the same for you. Here, come sit." She gestured toward the cluster of couches that served as their rooftop retreat. On the glass table were all the usual tidbits he loved, but today, they barely tempted him.

Maybe I'm just tired. It was *a long journey.*

"You've lost a lot of weight. Your face is so thin." She raised her hand to his cheek in concern. He flinched as her fingers grazed his skin. They were cold, so unlike the warm, delicate touch he remembered. "Are you feeling okay?"

"I am. I'm just a bit worn down from the runup to exams." He poured himself a draught from one of the expensive bottles in front of him. It was a vintage lucéat they only brought out on special occasions. Today no longer felt like that for Nate, but he downed it anyway.

Perhaps it'll set me straight.

"Well, we'll soon get you back to yourself again." She smiled at him and touched his hand, and in that moment, the world righted itself.

"Oh, Clara." He wrapped his arms around her and crushed her to his chest, breathing in her familiar scent as though it were the oxygen he needed to survive. "Clara." Here she was, his beautiful angel, his love.

What's wrong with me?

Perhaps she was right, and being away from her wasn't good for his health. But now he was home, where he belonged. With her.

She drew back, searching his face. "Are you *sure* you're okay?" Even her frown was elegant, and he almost laughed with joy.

"I am now. All I needed was to see your face, to feel you in my arms."

She stiffened, tempering the wildness of his joy and pulling all his old concerns to the surface.

Gently, Nate. You've got a few weeks. You've been away, so it's bound to be awkward at first. Just give her time. Not to mention, the last time they'd spoken, he'd hung up on her then refused to take any of her calls.

"Clara, about the last time we spoke—"

"Never mind about that. I'm sorry too. I said some things that maybe—"

"No! No, Clara. I'm glad you said what you did, even if it was wrong."

Her eyes widened and she leaned back as though to get a better view of him. "Wrong? What do you mean by *that*?"

"While I agree with what you said about all of us having a dark and a light side, I believe we would be fools to think we have a choice about it at all."

"You're calling me a *fool*?" Her brows drew together, signaling an impending storm.

"Of course not, Clara." He smiled indulgently. "I'm just saying that maybe you don't know as much as you think you do." The chance to finally teach *her* something was intoxicating.

A strong flush crept up her neck and bloomed in her face. It was a warning for him to stop, but he *needed* to educate her, to show her the truth of it. He couldn't let her live in ignorance any longer.

"You see, I think we have no control over these conflicting sides of ourselves. I think all this light, this dark—all our inspirations—are controlled by a higher power that exists apart from us and is beyond our comprehension."

She stared at him as though she couldn't grasp a word he'd just said. Good, the more baffling she found it, the more likely she would be to try to understand. Satisfaction burned warmly in his chest.

"I also believe that Coppelius was the first instance of this. He was a dark force I couldn't control then, just like I can't control whatever dark events happen to me now." *There. Let's see what she thinks about that.*

Her gaze had gone hard and her chin jutted out the way it had when they were children and she'd had enough of his and Loth's childish games. "What are you saying, exactly, Nate?"

"That I don't think we can control this darkness inside us at all, no more than we can control the light. We don't have the option to *accept* it. We have no choice but to surrender to it and live as it commands us." Calm slid smoothly through his veins. It was the truth.

She was having none of it. "You mean to say that you believe we should just accept the dark forces within us—and for the sake of argument, we'll ignore our differences on the source—and just let them destroy us?"

"There's nothing else we can do, Clara. Here." He handed her a tatty, worn notebook. "I've been writing down my thoughts on the issues, as well as some poetry. I know how much you enjoy it."

This is going better than I thought it would.

But Clara wasn't finished. "You think we should just give up and let the darkness consume us?"

"That's just the way it is." Hadn't she heard him? "Here, take it." He tossed the notebook onto her lap.

"I don't want to read your ridiculous ramblings." She shoved the book to the floor. "I can't believe I'm hearing this. I thought you going away would...would make you grow up and realize what was important in your life, who actually means anything to you." Her chest heaved as she tried to catch her breath around her anger. "But all you've done is found even more reason to be apathetic, because god forbid, you may actually be responsible for the things that happen in your life."

Her beauty drained from her face as she spoke, replaced by a haughtiness made all the more infuriating by her sudden plainness. How dare she speak to him like that, as ordinary as she was?

Nate leaped to his feet, slightly unsteady after the liquor. "You think you're so smart, Clara. But did it ever occur to you that maybe you're just cold-hearted? That what you think of as logic is just you imposing your will on others?" She stepped away from him, but he followed her, his annoyance heating into anger. She was going to listen to him, even if he had to hold her down. "You're ignorant of anything outside yourself, no matter how much you like to pretend otherwise. You'll never understand the real world and real people because you shut yourself up in this stupid tower, surrounding yourself with facts and reason, and judging the rest of us for following our true natures whenever they're not to your liking." He wagged a finger at her. "Yes, Clara, your heart is nothing but stone, I see that now. I see it..."

His eyes unfocused, and he stumbled over the leg of a chair. The jolt of pain as his knee hit stone shocked him, and he stared at her, his beloved Clara once more. What the hell was he doing? If anyone else had spoken to Clara like that, he would've flattened them. An apology was on the tip of his tongue before he caught himself.

No. I'm right. Every fiber of his being told him so. *And for the first time in my life, I don't care what Clara thinks.*

She would come around, and if not, well, then he wouldn't have to worry about any of the questions that had weighed him down for so long. She might choose to live in ignorance, but he wouldn't any longer. No, now *he* was the enlightened one.

She'd reached out a hand to steady him, but he brushed her off.

I have to get away from her.

Away from his fury and disappointment in her.

Grabbing the bottle that was supposed to celebrate his homecoming, he staggered back toward the elevator. If he stayed a minute longer, he would lose his nerve and break down, weeping, his arms around her waist and his face pressed against her as he abandoned what he now knew to be true, for what she believed to be right.

And I can't, not now when I finally understand. I've never seen the truth so clearly before.

His last glimpse of Clara was of her staring after him in shock, a breeze blowing the skirt of her dress around her knees and the sun reflecting the fire in her eyes.

EIGHT

It was awful. Clara had never read anything as tedious as Nate's journal. It was just more of the same nonsensical garbage. Things had been awkward ever since their conversation on the terrace, and Clara, unable to stand the tension any longer, had finally agreed to read through the dog-eared notebook, much to Loth's relief.

"Just read it, Clara," he'd urged later that night, after Clara told him what happened. Wild-eyed, he'd come to find her after listening to more than an hour of Nate's theories over several glasses of lucéat. "Please. Just humor him. It would mean a lot to him." He held the journal gingerly between two fingers, as though it were a bomb about to go off.

"What, and give his ridiculous ideas credibility? Why are you encouraging him?" She'd already wasted enough time humoring Nate's mother, who, of course, blamed his absence at the dinner table entirely on Clara.

"Clara…look, I know they sound crazy, and worse for you, illogical, but he's struggling right now and fighting with you is making things worse. He's only home for a few days. Read it, nod, smile, and then, when he goes back, you can burn it in effigy."

Why do I always have to be the one to give in?

It had been that way their entire lives. Her first thought was to throw the book back in Loth's face then lock herself in her office until Nate had gone home, but she couldn't. Her conscience was a curse.

"Fine." She'd taken the book and retreated to her room, determined to get it over with as soon as possible. She would read it, try to find something in it she could support, then she would go and make up with Nate.

But how could she, now that she'd seen what was in its pages? It was nothing but cringe-inducing, self-indulgent nonsense. Nate had always had an artistic temperament, so much so that when he'd announced he was planning to undertake a degree in business, Clara had almost choked on her cake. Loth, for all his self-indulgent behavior, had an acute business mind, and Clara had been doing scientific research since she was seven, helping her father untangle his newest theories.

Besides his talent with dreamscapes, Nate was a gifted painter and a skilled storyteller. His prose and poetry had been critically praised, and his future in the arts had seemed a sure thing. Why in the heavens he'd insisted on trying to be the Vice CEO of one of the biggest corporations in the Blackmoth was beyond Clara. Nate normally took Clara's advice into consideration, at least. But nothing she said could deter him. And Loth was useless, throwing up his hands when Clara asked for his help, merely saying that Nate had his reasons and she should learn to respect that.

The writing in his journal was devastating. All the sophistication, the nuances of language, the sparkling wit that was normally characteristic of his prose was gone. In its place was...well, she didn't really know what it was.

It waded through what he'd already told her about outside forces in painful detail then launched into what must be a poem, though Clara only guessed that from its format on the page.

It was an epic tale of the darkness Coppelius had thrust into Nate's life. It began with her and Nate, together, united by true love. Their bond was repeatedly attacked by a black hand, which reached in and out of their lives, yanking out the roots of any blossom of happiness which they enjoyed. This interference continued until a final showdown at the altar on the day of Clara and Nate's wedding.

Terrible old Coppelius appeared out of nowhere, evil incarnate, and laid his hands over Clara's eyes. They leaped from their sockets and onto Nate's chest, where they burned and sizzled, hissing and shooting a fountain of bloody sparks. Coppelius then grabbed Nate and threw him into a blazing circle of fire, which spun round and round like a tornado, until it carried him away over the ocean, causing the sea to rise to meet him in black, white-headed waves.

Throughout all of this, Clara's voice carried, crying out, "Can you not see me, dear? Coppelius has deceived you; they were not my eyes which burned so in your bosom; they were fiery drops of your own heart's blood. Look at me, I have my own eyes still."

And with this, Nate gained the power to grasp his fiery tempest in his hands and stop it then he scooped Clara up in his arms to kiss her, but when he gazed lovingly into her eyes, all he saw was death.

Bosom? Seriously?

It was ridiculous. Why had she let Loth talk her into reading it? How was she supposed to face Nate now and say nothing? God forbid she actually had to have a conversation with him about it. Before this, she would've been thrilled if Nate had written a poem about her, but this...she didn't even know what the hell this was. What was he trying to say with it? Whatever it was, it didn't seem to paint the relationship between them in a favorable light. Well, that was true enough right now. But it was Nate's doing, not Coppelius's.

Same old Nate—it's always someone else's fault.

She would just have to avoid him until he left. That was all there was to it.

She'd nested in a remote corner of the garden terrace, obscured by succulents and ferns. It was the only place she could think of where Nate wouldn't find her, unless she left the tower. She was going through some of her research when an alert pinged that another of Nate's dreams was in her inbox.

Ignore it.

Her resolve lasted for less than five minutes before she thrust her visor over her head and uploaded the dream.

She walked through tall grass along the edge of a lake, the leggy stalks catching and tugging at her hem. The sun shone down through the branches of the trees, and as the scent of baked marsh salt rose from under her feet, her heart was light. Damp stems licked at her hem and the soles of her feet like cool silk, pulling her down to the water's edge.

On the shore of the lake floated a small red and white wooden boat with satin-silver sails, dipping up and down with the gentle waves. The color of the water seemed to shift with each undulation, first the pale calm of cerulean then a troubled indigo to the midnight of loss and Nate's untidy hair. The boat was drawn by six shining white swans, each of which wore a plain golden crown and had a blue star painted on its forehead. As Clara's toes touched the edge of the water, the swans dipped their heads low in greeting, their wings curved into a curtsy. As she returned a deep bow to the birds, they fluttered their wings in consternation, calming only once she'd straightened and again towered over them.

Pacified, they inclined their delicate heads back toward the boat and waited. Clara climbed in and settled onto the pile of soft cushions padding the benches and set sail, the gossamer reins sliding gently between her fingers.

As they crossed the lake, gold and silver fish followed them, leaping high over her head in glittering masses before plunging deeply into the onyx water without even a ripple. Crimson-red and peacock-blue birds of all sizes followed the boat in formation as though escorting Clara on her voyage, trailed by fantastical iridescent plumage that stretched across the sky behind them like a meteor shower.

Her journey seemed to last forever, yet when she reached the other side, only an instant had passed. On the far shore bloomed a garden full of flowers—burnt-orange celosia, coral-pink dianthus, canary daffodils, and roses in every color. The breeze carried their scents to the traveler, a heady aroma warmed by the sun and sharpened with spices.

Palaces of cool gray marble and glass rose beyond the bank, sunlight rising from their shining turrets in a shimmering haze. On the shore stood a row of princesses, each cradling one of the small sugar pigs that had been Nate's favorite sweet when he was a child. All but one was dressed simply, in muted shades of fawn and dove gray, and as she watched, they crumbled the sugar between their fingers and let it fall into the water then licked the last bit of sweetness from their hands and turned away. Only one continued to face her, her expression haughty even through her lifeless eyes. She was resplendent in gold and pearl filigree, her auburn hair pulled tightly back from her face. As the boat got closer to shore, she stared Clara down then raised the sugar pig to her lips and bit off its head.

Clara had never seen her before, but Nate clearly had. Desire burned deep in Clara's belly, the longing to peel back the layers of the unknown and sample the enigmatic poison underneath.

Then her face became Clara's own, her dress of billowing white and dusted in pollen. The yearning in the pit of her stomach dissolved into a wish to see her smile, to hold her hand, to be near her in any way possible. Her heart was full to bursting, hope, happiness, and a profound sense of completion eclipsing everything else as the dream faded.

What the hell was all that? The love in her heart toward the end...and the hunger in it before that? The yearning for that cold queen, whoever she was. When she'd worn Clara's face, Nate had felt no yearning...only comfort, security. Embarrassment warmed her cheeks.

He doesn't think of me that way. As a woman he can't keep his hands off.

It stung, like an unseen cut suddenly touched with salt.

Well, it's not like you flaunt that side of yourself to him. Clara could never bring herself to put on a show of her sexuality—it just didn't feel natural—whereas that strange woman had exuded sensuality, even if Clara had thought her cold. Was she a real person? Or just a construct of Nate's mind? Clara had seen similar dreams before, in young adults who were crossing out of carefreeness of their youth into the expectations of adulthood. She wasn't sure who or what that other woman was supposed to represent, but then, not everything could be readily explained.

Maybe she'd underestimated how much Nate was struggling with these changes. When Clara and Loth had lost their parents at a young age, they'd entered adulthood prematurely but fairly easily. She'd assumed Nate had done the same. No wonder he hadn't spoken to her about it. He was probably worried about looking weak or immature in her eyes, though he should've known better.

No. She needed to give him the benefit of the doubt and support him through this, whether she agreed with his beliefs—and his hideous poetry—or not. She should tell him how much she admired him for who he was, how, to her, he would always be strong, kind, desired, and *loved*. Maybe it was time for *her* to accept some responsibility for *her* actions.

Perhaps if she'd told Nate how she felt about him before he went away, this never would've happened. He would've stayed here, done what was true to his nature, and they would've lived happily ever after.

But would they? That was only one possibility. What if all his teasing about their love was just that: a joke? What would happen if she had, in fact, declared her love for him? It was the same place Clara always returned to, the one step she'd never been brave enough to take.

So many times, it had been on the tip of her tongue, but something always seemed to get in the way. A new girlfriend, as far away in looks and temperament from Clara as possible. A reminder that their lives and business relationship were forever intertwined, though Nate would brush that off as inconsequential in the name of love.

But would he discount their friendship so lightly? Clara certainly didn't, and that was perhaps the biggest obstacle of all. If she admitted her true feelings and he didn't feel the same...she couldn't take it back. He would know, as would she, that she loved him in a way he couldn't reciprocate. Nothing would ever be the same. *Clara* would never be the same, and she wasn't too proud to admit that if that happened, she would make all their lives miserable. Where Nate was concerned, cool-headed pragmatism didn't exist.

The worst part was how honorable Nate was. Whether he loved her or not, he would marry her because he'd promised her father he would. Though many women would've been happy with that, Clara never could be, knowing that he was hers in name alone.

No. I want his entire heart and soul, or nothing at all.

Maybe it was time to fight for it.

***

Nate found her just as she was leaving the terrace.

"Clara? Can we talk?" His expression was uncharacteristically shy.

"Yes. Nate, I was looking for you. I wanted to—"

"I'm sorry, Clara. For the way I behaved the other night. I just...I was just trying to explain—"

She raised a hand to stop him. "I know. Here, come sit down." She led him over to the same snug in which they'd argued before. It was fitting to her, somehow, that they made up here too. His hand in hers was steady, and she smelled nothing on his breath. He was sober. Good. If they were to make it

67

through this conversation, they both needed to be as level-headed as possible.

"I saw your most recent dream, Nate."

"Really? I didn't think there was much to see. I can't really remember any of it. There was a boat and some swans...but that was about it."

Her heart dropped. So the way he'd felt about her in his dream...he didn't even remember. *Still, you know how his subconscious feels.* Bolstered again, she put her hand on his knee. "I don't think I've been as supportive of you as I could've been, Nate, and I'm sorry. You know me, the existence of anything I can't see or touch is hard for me to accept."

"I know. But you'll learn to open your mind in time." He patted her hand. "My dear Clara, still such a child in many ways, locked up here in this tower, knowing little of the real world."

What? What did he just say? Rage bubbled inside her, dark and molten.

After his apology, surely he could admit that he might've also gotten carried away, that these flights of fancy were just that, the result of a tired mind under pressure, unconsciously dragging up the past? His dreams and his reactions were so obvious, so easily explained by science and common sense, and yet here he was, still clinging stubbornly to the most obscure and unlikely of explanations.

Nothing had changed. *And* he'd confirmed that he still saw her as a...a *child*. Not a lover. Salt rubbed even deeper into the wound.

She shoved his hand away and stood up. "Are you serious, Nate? You still believe that some shadowy, mysterious force has gotten its hands on you? And that there's nothing you can do but succumb to its will like a helpless child?"

"I'm not succumbing, I'm merely accepting the darkness. Isn't that what you told me to do?" He smiled at her, a serene look that made her want to throttle him.

"No, Nate. I mean, yes, I did say to accept it, but in the sense that by accepting it, you take away the power it has over you, and you overcome it. *You* control it."

"But you can't, Clara." A wildness now shone in his eyes, a gleam Clara had never seen before. What was happening to him?

"Nate—"

"I thought I could make you understand. That's why I wrote the poem, Clara. For you. So you would finally *see*."

That was the last straw. "*The poem?* You should *burn* that poem, Nate. Burn the whole damn book. It's nothing but selfish nonsense."

"Selfish? But it's about you, Clara. About our love."

"Are you kidding me? Did you think that because you vomited some overwrought twaddle and slapped my name on it, I would be flattered? That might work on your floozies, Nate, but I'm not an idiot. I don't know what *you* think your poem says, but if that's how you see our 'love,' then...then..." Then what? Hadn't this been the moment she'd been waiting for? For him to admit he loved her? She did still love him, after all. She always would—it was her curse.

But not like this.

He stood and advanced on her, his hands shaking. "You're dead inside, Clara. You always have been. You're no more human than an android, than that elevator over there. You have no heart." His eyes flashed, like a strange and virulent fever had taken hold of him, and he gripped her shoulders with both hands, his fingers digging painfully into her flesh.

"Don't you dare touch my sister like that." In the heat of the moment, neither of them had noticed Loth approaching. "You may be my best friend, Nate, my brother, but Clara is my sister and the one person in the world I love more than you. And you will never touch her or speak to her like that ever again." In that moment, Clara's happy-go-lucky brother was gone, and there stood their father, resolute and unyielding, and Clara had never loved him more.

Nate rounded on him. "She is my betrothed, and she has to understand—"

He actually thinks of us as betrothed? I thought—

Loth flushed darkly. "No. She isn't. From this moment on, consider yourself *unbetrothed*. Now get out. You—"

Nate rushed him.

"Loth!" Clara was frozen. She watched helplessly as Nate bore down on her brother, and time seemed to slow. *Move, Clara, you have to help him.* Never in her life had she thought Nate and Loth would strike each other, but these weren't the men she knew.

She needn't have worried. Loth's fist connected with Nate's jaw in a perfectly aimed, furious swing, and Nate dropped like a stone.

Loth stared down at Nate's prone body then at his own fist then glanced up at Clara, the horror clear on his face. "Did I kill him?"

"I—"

Nate shuddered as he gasped and rolled over onto his back.

"I guess not. More's the pity." She glared down at him, suppressing the urge to land just one solid kick of her own.

"Clara? Loth? I—" He sat up, his expression of bewilderment making him look years younger. "What happened? I—" The confusion cleared, replaced by disbelief. He scrambled to his feet. "Clara, I'm so sorry. Please, forgive me. I...I don't know what came over me."

He seemed dazed, and Clara's heart relented. She wanted to be angry with him, to give him a taste of how badly he'd scared her. The physical pain had been nothing, but the idea that Nate, *her* Nate, could look at her with such fury, could assault her like she was nothing to him, that had left a mark.

But the look in his eyes now...not since they were children had she seen him so vulnerable. *This* was the Nate she'd fallen in love with, had daydreamed about marrying, had imagined growing old with.

"Oh, Nate." She pushed Loth aside and wrapped her arms around him. "What's gotten into you?"

He dropped his head to her chest "I don't know. I— Loth, please, I'm so, so sorry." A strangled cry forced itself from his throat and Loth hurried to embrace him, gathering both him and Clara in his trembling arms.

The three of them stood, holding each other on the top of the empire their parents had built, as they'd done when they were children and had given Bunty the slip during a storm. They would climb the secret staircase to the roof and huddle together, surrounded by the seething sky and buffeted by the furious wind. Against the squall they'd stood, their foundation of three solid and eternal, their hearts beating as one.

This was the closest to that memory they'd been in years. Each held on with all their might. A storm was coming—Clara felt it in her bones. But they would face it together, as they always had.

NINE

Three days after the incident on the terrace, Nate returned to university. The last few days had been happy ones, with everything almost back to normal, and even though Clara had still been a bit stiff with him, they were back on track. Yes, he still had some making up to do, but he'd boarded the boat for Draglight with his heart easier than it had been in months.

They'd all carefully avoided the subject of their disagreement for the rest of Nate's time at home. The ideas that had been so clear to him now seemed distant, and shame at the way he'd spoken to Loth and Clara, how he'd grabbed her, burned with an acrid sourness deep in his stomach. He wouldn't forget it anytime soon.

That's my punishment, to relive it over and over.

Nathanael disembarked on Draglight with a new purpose: get through the next semester and go home. Despite Loth and Clara's insistence that he had nothing to prove, he still wanted to see it through, and not just for Clara. No, it was time for him to take up his legacy. He squared his shoulders and waved to Sieg, who'd come down from the university to collect him.

"Sieg!" He clapped his friend on the back. "How are you? Have I missed anything? I—"

"Actually, Nate, you have." Sieg's face was uncharacteristically serious. "Our dorm burnt down."

Nate's travel case slipped from his fingers, hitting the pavement with a thump that scored the soft leather. "What do you mean, *burnt down?*"

"To the ground, my friend. All of it gone." Despite his solemnity, Sieg seemed impressed. "It went so quickly. I've never seen anything like it."

All his schoolwork…his possessions. His stomach twisted—that picture of Clara, the one next to his bed. He had copies of it somewhere, he was sure, but that portrait had been his talisman during his stay, had kept him focused. The depth of the loss took him by surprise. It was as though the fire had taken more than his belongings, leaving him adrift.

"Don't look so glum, Nate. No one was hurt, and we managed to save all your crap."

"You did?" *So why do I still feel like I lost something irreplaceable?*

"Of course." Sieg thumped him on the back again. "Come on, I'll take you to our new home."

"They've rebuilt it already?" Still dazed, Nate followed Sieg meekly, allowing the other man to carry his case.

"Of course not. No, they split us up into groups and moved us into houses in town. You and I have a house together, along with Marshall and Aadi. Unfortunately, we're across the street from old Spalazani, but the house is pretty nice." He opened the car door and ushered Nate inside. "And we each have our own bathroom. Imagine that, no more seeing Marshall's pasty ass first thing in the morning. Life is good, my friend."

Life is good.

Nate settled back as the car drew away from the curb, a measure of his balance restored. By the time they pulled up in front of the stately house that was to be their new dorm, he was no longer upset. This really was a much better situation. Not only were there the benefits Sieg had pointed out, but fewer drinking buddies in the mix meant he could concentrate more on his studies.

My new plan starts today—keep my head down, study hard, and get back to Clara as soon as possible.

Sieg showed him to his room then left to prepare for that evening's date. Nate brushed off his enthusiastic invitations, pleading tiredness from the journey and a desire to get settled back in.

When Sieg told him they'd rescued his things from the fire, he'd meant it—though much of the pile dumped in the middle of his room reeked of smoke, and smudges of ash covered nearly every surface. Still, gratitude made the mess irrelevant. Not everyone had people in their lives who would literally run through fire for them, and although he still couldn't shake his feelings of unease, disaster *had* been avoided.

For the next few hours, he painstakingly cleaned his things and restored them to their rightful places, until his room once again felt like a haven. It would be a fresh start, blotting out the trouble Vandran had brought to his door. The idea of a second chance reinvigorated him.

He opened the blinds, hoping to throw up the window and let in some fresh air to combat the smoky film that seemed to hang over everything.

And froze.

In the window directly across the road was Olympia. She sat as she always did, her head high, her expression fixed—right in his direction. For a moment, he was at a loss. What should he do? Should he wave? Or pretend he hadn't seen her?

He chose the latter, bustling around his room and occasionally stealing a glance in her direction. She was a striking woman, her face so classically and elegantly refined. Her shoulders were bare and creamy white, her skin flawless over the undulation of her collar bone. Her silky auburn hair had been set in one large curl that rested in a glossy coil over one of those delicate shoulders, and her eyes...her eyes... The room swirled around him, and he fell, senseless, his head narrowly missing the sharp corner of his desk.

Her eyes.

Her eyes? Whose eyes?

And what was so remarkable about them?

He glanced around. What was he doing on the floor? One minute he'd been looking out the window at Olympia across the street, and the next...

I must be more exhausted than I thought. He chuckled to himself. *If Clara saw me now, she'd have a fit. She told me I needed a few more days of rest, and she was right, as always.*

A sharp pang of loss for her and Loth struck him. *Perhaps I should send them a quick message, let them know I arrived safely.* He was turning over a new leaf, after all, and what better way to begin?

Pleased with himself, he sat down at his interface and poised his finger over the keys.

Something drew his gaze to the window again, to Olympia. He squinted. Was that a small smile curving her lips? No, she remained as stiff and humorless as always.

What a strange woman.

And how different from Clara.

I'm so lucky to have her in my life, even if it's not quite the way I want.

Clara. The portrait.

But despite how long he searched through the belongings his friends had saved, he couldn't find it. Clara's smiling face was gone.

TEN

Clara opened her eyes. She stood in an unfamiliar room, near an open window. The room, though comfortable, was sparsely furnished, and an acrid smell of smoke marred the air, though the room itself showed no signs of damage. A cool, fresh breeze beckoned to Clara through the window, and she bent to breathe it deeply in.

The coolness of the air came from the water, which had risen at some point during the night to cover all the streets and the lawn, rising until it lapped against the house with barely a foot to spare before it came through the window. Tiny goldfish flitted about in the midnight-teal depths like curious stars. They nibbled at Clara's fingertips and she laughed with joy, until a shadow fell over them and they darted away.

A long cherrywood boat pulled up next to the window, rowed by a dozen identical men. Eleven stared at her, their solemn faces crusted with salt, but the twelfth smiled and beckoned to Clara to board. Before she could decide, he was guiding her to a seat in the prow lined with embroidered cushions. The stylized eye of the Dreaming Life logo, stitched in glossy golden thread, pressed against her legs as the boatman shouted a command. They pulled away from the house with a cheer, breaking into song as they paddled between other celestial houses and into a great, open sea, dark and fathomless as the night sky.

Clara reclined against the soft pillows, a wave of calm contentment washing over her. The steady rhythm of the rowers soothed Clara, and she'd nearly dozed off when her boat was joined by a flock of pearl and onyx storks, the breadth of their wings appearing to cover the sky. Or were they in the water? The boat seemed to float in nothingness, neither sky, nor ocean, and yet onward the men rowed, their oars dipping gently into the heavenly ether. The great birds flew alongside in a line that stretched back, too far for Clara to see the end.

Under her gaze, one of the storks faltered and fell out of line. It spread its wings and wafted gently down, like a divine feather, to land next to Clara on the prow of the boat. The poor thing was exhausted, and Clara gathered it in her arms then placed it on the floor of the boat so it could rest. It lifted its face to hers then raised its wings, obscuring anything beyond.

The boat shuddered, and for a moment, even the nothingness disappeared. The rowers froze in place, their oars suspended uselessly in the air, their faces fixed in determined expressions.

Something was wrong. Dreams did not suddenly freeze like this, they—

The oars swung back and forth again, one rower shouting out the rhythm to the others. Cool, moist air bathed Clara's face, wafting gently on her cheeks from the beating of the flock's wings.

The stork on the floor of the boat had turned into a woman.

She rose to her feet, standing before Clara in all her glory. She wore nothing but the auburn hair falling loosely about her milky shoulders, and her green eyes shone, enraptured, as they gazed at Clara with a desire that made her gasp.

Something unfurled in Clara then, a dreamy warmth behind her eyes that flowed down through her body, heating her lips and curling around her heart. She gazed back at the angelic creature, awe holding her breathless. Fire rose deep in her belly, and her hands ached to explore the—

The woman Nate had feelings for. Passionate feelings. Feelings he didn't have for Clara.

The woman smiled, a strange, slightly crooked smile, as though she was still learning how. The strangeness only made her more ethereal; perhaps Clara had been smiling the wrong way her entire life.

"Keep rowing! Faster!" The startling voice was Clara's.

She turned from the woman to find that each of the rowers now wore her face, her body. Her expression was still determined, but with a new hardness that made her features callous, and her body was bent and twisted, the fingers around the oars too long and sharp.

Like fiends the Claras rowed, faster and faster, and icy dread rose from the pit of her stomach when she looked at their impish faces. She didn't want to go where they were taking her. Her body shook, trying to rebel, to escape.

She had to get out, now.

The lovely woman laid a hand on Clara's arm, and the warmth melted her panic, suffusing her with a sweet hope and offering her something even better—freedom. She reached out to Clara, and as their fingers touched, a pain so sublime it brought tears to Clara's eyes split the skin on her back and she sprouted wings, every bit as grand as the storks above her. Clara and her savior took to the air, soaring high and away from both the line of storks and the boatful of Claras.

Her happiness rose with her.

That was what she truly wanted, had wanted all along. She just hadn't known it.

Clara yanked the visor off her head and slammed it down onto her desk. What the hell was going on inside Nate's head? Her cheeks burned.

You know the answer.

Nate saw a future with her and their legacy at Dreaming Life as a journey he didn't want to take—because of her. He saw her as an evil taking him somewhere he didn't want to go, and he saw this other woman, whoever she was, as his saving grace, his escape from Clara.

I knew things still weren't right between us.

Nate's visit had ended much better than it started, but even though they'd all kissed and made up, things were *not* back to normal, despite Loth's insistence. Nate had behaved the same way he always did, placating both his mother and Loth, but he hadn't fooled Clara. No, it was though part of him was still changed, though so subtly she couldn't explain it.

Until this dream. Did he still intend for her to see his dreams, knowing he might dream of this other woman? If so, why would he want her to know? Did he suspect the depth of her feelings for him and was trying to let her down? Or had he forgotten that he'd given her access in the first place? Well, she certainly wasn't going to remind him. It did feel slightly unethical to keep viewing his dreams without double-checking with him first, but he *had* given her permission.

Besides, something was going on with Nate, something beyond his feeling for another woman, and she needed to find out what it was. If it was just that he felt trapped in the future plotted out for him, that was one thing. Yes, it would devastate her, but it would *kill* her if he went through with living a lie. She loved Nate too much to force him into a life he didn't want, no matter how selfishly she wanted it to be different.

She dropped her head into her hands. That other woman. Who was she? She seemed familiar, but was she someone Nate knew in waking life, or was she a figment, his mind's recreation of his perfect woman and what she represented to him? Was she—

Clara *had* seen her before—in Nate's previous dream. The sugar-pig princess.

But how did she relate to his real life? And how could Clara find out without tipping him off? Shame pricked at her, but she brushed it off. Their betrothal may never have meant anything, but they did own a business together. She had a right to know if he was hiding something, especially if that something was the real object of his affections. Clara's personal heartbreak aside, Dreaming Life's future security might depend on it.

She nodded to herself, satisfied. She would come up with a plan.

He's right, you are a robot.

"No, I'm not." Nate's words had stung, but she'd known in her heart, despite what Nate said, that it wasn't true. She was just practical.

Being able to compartmentalize doesn't make you heartless. It helps you to survive.

The reminder wasn't as much a relief as she'd thought.

You can't let him get to you. You know what's in your heart, Clara, and now you can find out what's in his.

That made her feel better.

Besides, there were more issues with his dream than his feelings. A problem she hadn't seen before. She checked her records—none of the other researchers on any of the other dream projects had reported any incidences of a dream freezing before. Normally, dreams were like giant rivers—unstoppable, quick to find a way around any obstacle in their paths. What had happened to her in Nate's dream wasn't supposed to happen. Shouldn't have been *able* to happen.

But who could she talk to about it? Not Loth. His eyes glazed over whenever she talked about her research; sometimes she wondered if he even knew what she did. One of the other researchers? Too risky. If they found out the subject was Nate, they could leak it to the public. It had to be someone she could trust implicitly, someone who had the best interests of Dreaming Life at heart.

So who? The answer was clear, but still she cast about, hoping there was another one, *any* other one, that would be just as viable.

There wasn't.

She sighed. Well, it would be better to get it over with. She opened the bottom drawer of her desk and pulled out the lucéat Loth had hidden there for when he came to visit her. She swigged it straight from the bottle, wiping her mouth as a bit of the golden liquid escaped and trickled down her chin.

That was better. She stashed the bottle back in its hiding place then stood. She could do this. For their future.

For Nate.

***

As she knocked on Arienne's office door, the lucéat curdled in her stomach. Ugh. Why had she done that? Any courage it had given her dissipated at the squeak of Arienne's chair as she rose from it to answer the door.

There was a pause then the door opened just enough to reveal Arienne's thin, pallid face, her hollow eyes boring through Clara and her hairless brows raised in expectation. Her mouth quirked on one side when she saw Clara and she stepped back, inclining her head to usher her in.

"Miss Clara, what a lovely surprise." Clara had asked all their staff to call her by her first name, hoping it would foster a sense of community, but Arienne insisted on calling her Miss.

She closed the door behind Clara and gestured to one of the chairs in front of her desk. As she circled back to her chair, Clara sat and watched her unhurried progress.

There was something odd about Arienne she'd never been able to put her finger on. She'd worked at Dreaming Life for years, before her father's death, before he and Nate's father had taken on the company it would eventually become. Her credentials were impeccable, and her father had been thrilled when they'd recruited her. "That woman has an exceptional mind," he'd said. "We definitely want her on our side." And so she had been, ever since.

Perhaps it was the way she looked, all angles and sallow skin, her pastel blue eyes set deep in her narrow, almost gaunt, face. Maybe it was her lack of eyebrows, which gave her an otherworldly look. Clara had often considered asking her what had happened to her eyebrows, but she generally tried to avoid asking her anything. It was a mistake she'd made once, and after Arienne's long-winded, tangent-filled explanation, she'd sworn she'd never do it again.

And maybe that was the problem. She was incredibly pedantic, even for a scientist, and during staff meetings, the other scientists visibly winced whenever she cleared her throat and raised her hand. They also never seemed to invite her to any of their after-work get-togethers, but Clara doubted she'd even noticed. Or if she did, she certainly didn't care.

But Clara's father had been right about her mind. Arienne's area of research focused on patient acceptance, making the elements of their reality seamless enough that they accepted it without question. It was very delicate work and required a deep understanding of the flow of the dream state. If anyone knew how a glitch could occur in a natural dream, it was her.

Finally settled in her chair, she appraised Clara. "Is there something wrong, Miss Clara? Something with my work?" She looked faintly displeased, as though Clara had already leveled several baseless accusations at her.

"No, Arienne, of course not. Your work is impeccable, as always."

Placated, she leaned back in her chair and steepled her fingers under her chin. "What can I assist you with, then?"

Clara squirmed under her gaze. Why did Arienne make her so uncomfortable? "It has to do with my own research."

"Ahh." Her pale eyes gleamed and she leaned forward in anticipation. "Please, go on."

She recounted Nate's dream, carefully leaving out much of the detail, especially that it was a personal study, *not* an official one. The less said about that, the better. "For a few seconds everything just...froze. Then when it started up again, things were different. I've never seen anything like it."

"And what do you think it has to do with me?" Her tone was sharp.

"Well, nothing. I just thought you might've heard of this phenomenon before." Was *she* this prickly with people? Was she, right now, talking to future Clara?

Somewhat mollified, Arienne sighed. "I see." She tilted her head back and stared at the ceiling. Clara's heart sank. When Loth imitated Arienne, that was invariably how he began, his eyes to the heavens before launching into an overly detailed tirade that made Clara want to claw her eyes out and stuff them in her ears. She was in for a long one. Hopefully, it would be worth it.

For Nate. Yes. Anything would be worth it for Nate.

She waited patiently as Arienne nodded to herself then angled her head back to meet Clara's eyes. "I don't think it's anything."

Clara waited for her to say more, but Arienne merely folded her hands on top of her desk and gazed at her benignly. "What? That's it?"

Arienne's hairless brow furrowed. She seemed confused by Clara's bewilderment. "Yes. I'm sorry. Were you hoping for a different answer?"

Yes. That this was a massive glitch with my equipment and the dream was wrong. That Nate is actually wildly in love with me and not some other woman. "No, I'm just perplexed. Have you seen anything like this before?"

"Yes. I'm surprised you haven't, to be honest." Her voice was neutral, but it still rankled. "Don't worry, Miss Clara." Arienne reached out and patted her hand.

Given the way she looked and her legend in the company, Clara expected the touch of her hand to be revolting, soft and clammy. But it was warm and dry, and surprisingly comforting. In fact, it reminded her of her mother, and she suppressed the urge to snatch it up, press it to her face, and tell her everything.

"I just—"

"It's much more likely to be a problem with your equipment than the subject." She paused then fixed her keen gaze on Clara again. "May I ask who the subject is? Just for context, of course." Her eyes glittered.

Should I tell her? It might be easier if she could explain in greater detail. But not only was it a personal thing between her and Nate, he was also, technically, this woman's boss. It was too much of a conflict of interest.

"I'm sorry, Arienne, that information is strictly private. The patient's wishes."

Arienne inclined her head in acknowledgment, but the corner of her mouth twitched downward. "As you wish."

"You've been tremendously helpful, already," Clara lied and rose from her chair. "I'll rerun the dream with some different equipment and see if it happens again. If it does, you'll be the first to know."

The other woman brightened at that and pushed her own chair back. "Thank you for coming to me,

Miss Clara. I admired your father tremendously, and it's an honor to serve you as well."

It was an odd way to put it, but Clara just nodded. "Thank you, Arienne, I know my father had a lot of respect for you."

The moment Arienne's office door was closed, Clara sprinted down the hallway, past the bewildered stares of the other researchers.

Could Arienne be right? Could it be something as mundane as faulty equipment? It just seemed too easy; she'd expected Arienne to be shocked, or at least surprised. Somehow, the glitch felt much more sinister than a simple technical fault.

Nate's rubbing off on you. Now you're starting to see shadows lurking in every corner. Get it together, girl.

The last thing she needed was to buy into Nate's hysteria. That wouldn't help either of them. No, the problem was nothing supernatural; no dark power was acting against her. Like Arienne had said, it was probably just an issue with the equipment.

There was one way to find out. Clara splashed some cold water on her face, squared her shoulders, and marched back into her office. She retrieved another visor, this one straight out of the box, hooked it up to her system, and slipped it on.

Half an hour later, she pulled the visor off her head. Arienne had been right—it must've been a hardware issue. This time, when Clara had relived Nate's dream, there was no glitch. A seamless, infuriating visit into Nate's psyche. What had she been hoping for?

That the glitch meant the whole thing was a mistake? That on the second run-through it wouldn't be the strange woman's face that Nate gazed adoringly at, but her own? That Nate would row into his future at Dreaming Life with enthusiasm? If so, she was sorely disappointed.

Before she could stop herself, she snapped the visor in her hands. *Damn.* Good thing she was the boss—and that Loth couldn't care less about inventory. Something about the dream still bothered her, but she couldn't pin it down. Was it just that Nate's fascination with that woman hurt her feelings? Or was something genuinely amiss? Either way, she would have to wait for his next dream to find out.

ELEVEN

"Hey, lovely." Nate crossed one leg carelessly over the other and draped his arms over the back of his chair. *"How are you? I know it's been a few days since my last message, but that's because I've been studying. I know, right?"* He gave a throaty laugh and leaned forward toward the camera. *"You've probably fallen off your chair in shock. But there you have it. I'm determined to ace these exams and make you and Loth look bad when I come back from the Draglight with a spanking-new diploma. I'll be the first person in the family with a business degree."* Smugness tugged at the corner of his mouth. Loth wouldn't be able to stand it.

"Now, I know you've got a birthday coming up—you thought I'd forget, didn't you?" He wagged a finger at the recorder. *"I thought we should do something special. I've got one or two ideas, but I'm going to talk to Loth about them first. But I do have a special present planned—you're going to love it."* A sharp knock sounded on his door, three raps in quick succession.

"Anyway, there's someone at the door, so I'm going to love you and leave you, but I'll message again soon, I promise!" He made a cross over his heart and grinned.

"Take care, and keep me in your heart." He pressed his fingers to his lips and hit send. There. Now Clara couldn't complain that she hadn't heard from him.

"Come in!" Nate switched off his screen and rubbed his hands together in anticipation. He'd commissioned a custom piece for Clara's birthday, and he wanted every detail to be just right. As such, he'd spared no expense, bringing in one of the top coral crafters in the country from the famed Winternola Atoll to create a one-of-a-kind jewelry box.

But it wasn't just a birthday gift. The coral box would hold his parents' engagement ring. Hopefully, Clara would love it, and it would give him the courage to finally take the risk and propose. It was a drastic step, and maybe he would've been wiser to get a better handle on how she actually felt first, but after everything that had happened lately, a grand gesture was needed.

He spun around in his chair and his heart nearly stopped.

The man hovering in the doorway wasn't the coral crafter. Vandran had returned.

Fire roared in Nate's ears as he leaped to his feet. *Now we've got eyes—a beautiful pair of children's eyes.* Vandran's image seemed to stretch and widen, his green eyes glittering like sharp-cut emeralds, his skin the sickly yellow of the dying.

He held out his revolting, hairy hands to Nate, crying, "We've got eyes! We've got eyes!"

Nate staggered, slamming his lower back against the edge of his desk. Winded, he slumped down in his chair, limp and aching with fear.

It's not Coppelius. It's not Coppelius. Clara's voice rose up to quench the fire.

"It's not him. That man is not Coppelius."
She was right. Clara was always right.
Just think of Clara, your guardian angel.
Clara.
The roaring dulled and receded, as did the specter of Coppelius. It left only Vandran behind, his thin face creased in amusement, his green eyes boring into Nate's soul. In his outstretched hands, he cradled a steel case. "Sir? Are you all right?"

"I—" Nate dropped his hands and drew a shuddering breath. *It's not Coppelius. There is no dark force. You're bringing this on yourself.* "Yes, thank you. I just stood up too fast." He glared at the dealer. "I thought I told you I didn't want any of your crap."

"Did you? I'm sorry, sir, but have we met before? This is first time I've been to this address."

Did he not remember Nate? Was it a trick? Was he— Nate caught himself. *Of course.* He'd been in the dorms when Vandran came to him the first time, so why would the man remember him? He probably saw dozens of students and faculty members a day, hundreds and thousands during the weeks and months as he traveled around Foxwept.

Because he's not Coppelius, and he doesn't know you.

"Professor Spalazani said you'd moved on." His breathing was almost back to normal, though his heart still pounded in his chest.

"That is true enough, but that was a few weeks ago, I believe. I do rotations, you see."

"I understand. I—"

"Would you like to see my wares? I've got all sorts. Preprogrammed VR in visors or chips, lenses that change your eye color, whatever a young man might fancy." He slammed the case down on Nate's table, opening it and pulling out an assortment of goods.

"Wait, stop! I said I didn't want anything."

"Would you not even like to look?"

"No, I don't need anything. I—"

"Well, if not for you, perhaps for a family member? A friend? Someone with a special occasion like a birthday?"

Clara's birthday *was* coming up. And though he was giving her the ring, something amusing before that would be fun. *Imagine her face.* "Do you have anything for a young woman?"

Vandran pondered for a moment then drew a black visor edged with rose gold out of the pile. "This item may interest you. It shows the viewer things as they truly are."

It was a con, of course. How could that possibly work? Still, it did fit the bill for a lighthearted gift, especially for someone as serious as Clara.

He might as well humor the man and try it out. He could always say no. Plus, he'd be able to recount the story to Clara—*omitting the first part where I was terrified, obviously*—and satisfy her concerns about his preoccupations with dark forces and Coppelius. Here he was, facing his fear while remaining calm and civil.

Nate raised the visor to his eyes. It was a bit too small for him but that didn't matter, because— A blinding pain seared into his brain, as if his eyeballs had been pierced by thousands of tiny pins. He gagged and clawed at the visor, but it had welded fast to his face, and he dropped to his knees in agony. The dark force which he'd dismissed reared its head again, taunting him with a guttural laugh and layer on layer of agony. Clara had been wrong. So very, very wrong, and now he was going to die.

Just as he began to pass out, the visor was wrenched from his face and Vandran peered down at him, his eyes wide and his mouth hanging open in surprise.

"Sir? Are you okay? Can you speak?"

Nate tried but his tongue felt too big for his mouth, and all he could push out was a few garbled syllables. Vandran reached out to help him up, but as soon as Nate accepted, he recoiled in horror at the feel of the others man's skin, moist and soft, like the hand of a drowned corpse. Nate snatched his hand away and scrambled to his feet, still trying to find his voice.

When he finally did, it came out rasping and hoarse, his throat burning as though he'd been screaming in hell for all eternity. "What did you do to me?"

"Sir?" Vandran held out both his hands to show his innocence. "Nothing. It was the visor, though I've never seen anything like it before. I'm so sorry." He stuffed the visor into his pocket. "I'll notify the company right away, send it back to them for inspection."

"Let me look at it." Nate's voice was commanding in its roughness, and the optics dealer winced.

"I'm sorry, sir, but—"

"Give it to me!" Nate grabbed for the man's pocket, but Vandran danced away then pulled the visor out and crushed it in his hands.

"Why did you do that?"

"Company policy, sir. If an item is defective, it must be destroyed immediately."

"But you just said you were going to send it back to them."

"Yes, *after* I rendered it unusable."

"I…I…" The room around Nate spun again.

"Here, sir, please sit down before you fall again."

Nate let Vandran help him to his chair, recoiling at his touch even through the fabric of his sleeve. This man revolted him, though he didn't know why. What had he been upset about? Something about a visor? Why was he so dizzy? He sat dumbly for a moment then turned to the dealer. "What happened?"

He looked at Nate appraisingly then gathered his goods and arranged them neatly back in the case. "I came by to see if you wanted to buy an optic, my young sir." He closed the case with a snap. "But I don't think I have anything you'd be interested in."

"What's your name?" If Nate could get his name, maybe he could remember who the man was and why he was vaguely afraid of him.

"Vandran, sir. Gordon Vandran. I'm an optics dealer from…"

The man's voice faded as Nate searched his memory. Vandran? It was a different name, but recognition of *something* danced just beyond his reach. *Think, Nate. Think.* He looked out of his open window and the world spun again, but this time its dizzying whirl was intoxicating. Glorious, even. Sitting at the window across from him was the most perfect creature he'd ever seen.

Olympia.

He'd seen her before, of course, many times. But never before had her cold beauty seemed so radiant. How had he resisted running his fingers through that fiery mane? Stroking that rose-tinted, alabaster cheek, so delicate it made him want to weep? How would her divine figure feel in his arms, that long, graceful neck under his lips?

And her eyes.

Her eyes.

How had he not noticed how lovely her eyes were? He'd once thought them fixed and lifeless, but he couldn't have been more wrong. An azure blue so pure it put the sea and sky to shame, shot through with the silver of glittering moonbeams...they made him breathless. Passion for her filled him, a passion that grew every second he looked at her. How could he have been so blind?

I have to talk to her. He would throw himself at her feet and beg for her forgiveness that he'd overlooked her, that he only now saw what an extraordinary woman she was.

A cough and the shuffling of feet behind him interrupted his rapture. The man, Vandran, still stood behind him, waiting patiently for his attention.

"What are you still doing here?" Nate let his irritation show. The sooner Vandran left, the sooner Nate could get back to admiring Olympia. Taking his eyes off her for even a moment had threatened to open a void in his soul.

Vandran followed his gaze to the window and let out a low whistle. "Now there's a fine-looking woman—"

Nate's hands were around the man's throat before he could finish. "Get out. And don't you dare so much as look at her again. She is a goddess, and you're nothing but common trash."

Vandran seemed indifferent to Nate's insult. He carefully disengaged himself from Nate's grip and sidled to the door. "Okay, then. Have a good afternoon, sir."

Nate caught the smirk on his face as he passed out the door, and the desire to chase after Vandran, to grab him again and force him to his knees in front of the lovely Olympia burned in his chest. *Make him grovel for daring to look at her.* But he couldn't bear to turn away from her for a second more.

He raced back to his window.

But she was gone.

Anger and disappointment overwhelmed him, and he snatched up the closest thing to hand and threw it to the floor, satisfied by the shattering of glass. He had to get out, go for a walk and clear his head. *Or maybe she's out taking a walk too.* Yes. That had to be it.

He rushed out to meet her, forgetting his shoes and slicing open the bottom of his foot on the remains of Clara's new portrait, now nothing but a distant memory and a few bloodstained shards.

TWELVE

Clara was ready to explode as she checked her messages for the hundredth time.

Nothing.

Neither she nor Loth had had a message from Nate for days. In the last one she'd received, he'd seemed to be feeling better—almost like the old Nate. And yet, according to Loth, Nate hadn't spoken to him about whatever plans he had for Clara's birthday.

I wonder what my special present is. Obviously, there was something she *hoped* for, but that was all it was likely to be—hope. The chances of Nate getting down on one knee and proposing were slim to none. But still, Clara could dream, couldn't she?

And speaking of dreams, not only had there been no messages from him, but no significant dreams, either. Just jumbled collages of studying intercut with images of eyes. Clara couldn't help feeling that the eyes maybe meant something, but the flashes were so brief and random, she couldn't make out what that might be.

Should she send him another message? No. *I don't want to look desperate.* If he hadn't replied to the first two, why would he respond to a third? He was probably, as he'd said in his last message, studying for his exams. That should've thrilled her, but it didn't.

I'm just never happy, am I?

She squinted at the clock. 3 a.m. Ugh. Definitely time for bed. Should she check her messages one last time?

Her message alert pinged just as she was about to open her client, startling her. Her heart leaped in her chest as she saw it was another of Nate's dreams. *Don't get excited. The last one was an hour of staring at a test screen.* She glanced at the clock again. It wasn't *that* late.

Her fingers trembled as she slipped on her visor. Would this dream give her some clue to what was behind Nate's silence? Would there be another glitch?

The smell of incense was almost overpowering, a heady mix of orris and orange blossom that was unfamiliar and unwelcome. Clara pressed the back of her hand to her nose as she peered through the haze. Where am I? The strains of an orchestra rose unobtrusively above the chatter of the crowd, mingling with the chimes of laughter.

The room was ornately decorated, festooned with oversized white orchids and dripping with gaudy silver garlands. It was also packed full of people, each more glamorous than the last. All wore red, the traditional color of wedding parties in the higher echelons of Foxwept.

Why was Nate dreaming about a wedding? Whose wedding was it? Was he reliving one they'd already been to?

I hope not. Weddings were tedious enough in real life.

She glanced around at the men surrounding her. If she could recognize anyone, it might give her a clue. Inside, Nate's nervousness grew, a sense that he would simply vanish, evaporating cell by cell in the heat of this celebratory inferno.

On their side of the room, the women giggled and threw sparkly confetti over each other until they glittered, while the men stood stoically in midnight-black suits accentuated by bloody crimson, as though guarding a flock of particularly prized birds. Their movements seemed strangely exaggerated, their smiles too wide, their teeth too white, their fingers too long and grasping.

Clara glanced down at her hands, turning them over. Nate's normal hands, the nails bitten to the quick, the scar on the back from when six-year-old Loth had brought a stray dog home.

A sigh burst from Nate's chest as the crowd of women parted slightly, and Clara glimpsed a quantity of swirling white taffeta and chiffon, alternately smoothed and fluffed by the exotic creatures whirling around it.

The bride. A white rose in a sea of blood.

Clara stood on her tiptoes to get a better look. Nate's anticipation squeezed her throat, making it hard to breathe. Many hands suddenly pressed into her back, pushing her forward into the center of the room. The men stepped back, giving her a wide berth, and all eyes focused on her.

The bridegroom. This was Nate's wedding.

The bride approached her groom, flanked on both sides by giggling handmaidens. Her face was obscured by an elaborate ivory veil that hung to the floor over her demurely bowed head. Once next to Nate, she linked her arm with his and raised her covered face to the crowd.

The crowd pressed the couple forward. More and more people poured into the room until it was as full as a rabbit warren, the air stale and stifling. The bride and Nate had been pushed from the center of the throng to stand in front of the only exit; their guests were trapped.

Nate grasped the hem of his bride's veil with shaking hands and lifted it, revealing her face. There was a swift intake of breath all around the room, murmurs of approval that rippled outward, turning into cheers by the time they reached the people against the walls.

It was the woman from his other dreams, the haughty beauty with auburn hair. She smiled at him, a smile devoid of any warmth or love, little more than a blood-red cut across her porcelain skin.

Nate was dreaming about marrying another woman.

Nausea gripped Clara's stomach, both her and Nate's. He was about to throw up, sickness and dread curling up from his stomach to leave a bitter, metallic taste in his mouth. And yet, a wild joy bubbled under the bitterness, a too-honeyed tang.

In fact, all the emotions rolling off him were contradictory and volatile. He was drawn to the other woman with the fervor of an acolyte, but this passion was rivaled by his fear of her. One minute, his heart soared to unimaginable heights, the next it plunged into deep, suffocating darkness.

Clara's heart rose and fell, bled and beat with each of these sensations until she thought she could no longer bear it. Nate's will, his ability to control himself, seemed to grow more tenuous, more insubstantial. Even in his dream he appeared to feel it, raising his hands to cover his eyes and uncover them again as the crowd surged around them.

His heart beat rapidly, a thunder in his chest that resonated through the wedding chamber as the crowd cheered and threw streamers and more confetti. Nate's eyes bulged from his head and he clutched at his chest. His bride merely smiled, her face cool and composed as her husband-to-be fell to his knees by her side. He ripped open his shirt, as though escaping his clothes would end this spectacle.

Nate dropped his head and Clara stared at his chest. The tattoo over his heart was missing.

Had it been gone in the other dreams? She couldn't remember—she hadn't been looking for it.

When people dreamed, the smallest details about them were incorporated into their dreams whether they realized it or not. Even sickness and pain usually followed them, which was what Dreaming Life had been created to circumnavigate.

Nate's tattoo should've been there, the three stars, shining and immortal, that represented him, Clara, and Lothair. What did its absence mean?

Agony twisted Nate's mouth, an anguish that seared her very soul. His heart blazed its way out of his chest, the embers swirling around him and scorching his skin, and his bride tossed back her head and laughed with joy.

Clara had seen enough. Reluctantly, she left Nate to burn at his own wedding and switched off her visor. Her chest still stung, as though an errant spark had followed her back to reality.

She had no idea what the missing tattoo meant, but it could be a clue to whatever was happening with Nate.

Perhaps Arienne would know. The older woman had been confident that the glitch in Nate's dreams had been nothing more than that—a glitch. But this, this was something else, something concrete. Something that *definitely* shouldn't have been there. Or rather, *should've* been. Clara rubbed her temples.

Clara, Dreaming

Before she called Arienne, she was going to check Nate's other dreams and see if his tattoo was there. She had no idea what it meant either way, but it was a start.

***

"And then it disappears, sometime during the glitch." She was talking too fast, but she couldn't help it, and besides, Arienne didn't seem to mind.

The older woman sat at Clara's desk with her fingers over her mouth, nodding as Clara pointed out her discovery. "I agree, I think it means something too."

"Do you have any idea what?" Now that she'd found some kind of clue, Clara was anxious to speed up their investigation. Whatever was happening to Nate seemed to be getting worse.

Is this why I haven't heard from him? I should've done something sooner.

But it was no good scolding herself; it wouldn't change anything. Besides, she'd likely be just as upset if she *had* done something before she'd had any clues.

Ari leaned back in her chair and sighed. "I have a pretty good idea, but..."

"But what?"

"It sounds a bit...outlandish."

"Well, that definitely describes Nate's behavior lately." She winced and bit the inside of her cheek. *Damn.* So much for keeping Nate's secret.

Ari, however, took it in a stride. "Well, if these dreams are unnatural, that doesn't surprise me."

"Please, tell me whatever it is you know." Thinking something was wrong with him and *knowing* was the difference between concern and outright panic.

"Someone is manipulating Mr. Nathanael's dreams."

"What?"

"Exactly what I said. Someone has somehow hacked into Mr. Nathanael's dreams, and is manipulating them." Ari leaned back and crossed her arms over her chest.

"But how could they even do that?"

"Does Mr. Nathanael have any implants?"

"Yes. He's got a Dreaming Life VR chip—all three of us do. We had them put in so we could test our programs personally."

"Hmmm. I suppose it's possible. But the security on them is pretty tight, isn't it?"

"Oh, yes. They're unhackable. Besides, we'd see evidence if anyone had tampered with them."

"Does he have anything else?"

"An optic chip that makes him see color."

"Mr. Nathanael's color-blind?" Ari's eyes narrowed.

Clara nodded. "Ever since he was a child."

Ari considered then shook her head. "That type of chip wouldn't be powerful enough. Not for this kind of manipulation."

"How can you tell? The manipulation, I mean." It was fascinating. Dream forensics was high up on Clara's to-do list for the future of Dreaming Life.

"It's very good work—but it's not perfect. Not for someone of *my* experience." She grinned at Clara.

Clara smiled back. Some might have thought Ari was being arrogant, but it was simply the truth and Clara appreciated a woman who claimed her accomplishments.

Ari continued. "On its own, the glitch may have been nothing. But when combined with the missing tattoo, it's *something*. Whoever is manipulating Mr. Nathanael's dreams doesn't know about his tattoo."

"Wouldn't Nate's mind simply fill it in, though, the way it does in regular dreams?"

Ari grunted. "I'm glad you're not just accepting what I say without questioning it. Good girl." She leaned back and stared at the ceiling, only this time, Clara couldn't wait to hear what she had to say.

"There could be several reasons his brain isn't overlaying it. One is that whomever is interfering is being too heavy-handed and his mind simply can't push through. Or it could be that his consciousness is simply too confused to insert it. Or," and she dropped her chin to her chest and stared at Clara, "it could be Mr. Nathanael sending out a cry for help."

Clara pressed her hands to her mouth. It had been bad enough when she'd thought Nate was party to these dreams, but the thought that not only were they against his will, but that he *knew* and was crying out for help...it was all she could do not to run up to the company heliopad and hijack one to fly to Draglight and rescue him.

"Miss Clara, get a hold of yourself." Ari's expression was stern. "Going to pieces isn't going to help anyone."

Clara lowered her hands and held them behind her back, and Ari nodded in approval.

"That's better. Now, there were other dreams that he sent you? Like the one you first came to me with?"

"Yes. This is the third...strange one. The first one he sent me was completely normal, as far as dreams go."

"Can I see them, please? It might help me to figure out a pattern."

"Of course." Clara didn't hesitate. Less than a minute later, Clara watched as Arienne explored Nate's dreams, her frown deepening with each successive vision. When she was finished, she turned to Clara and sighed. "There's good news and bad news."

"What's the good news?" How could there possibly be any?

"Whoever is behind this is getting desperate. There's little symbolism in this dream, which means the manipulator has given up on subterfuge and is trying to force Nathanael to take action as quickly as possible."

"That sounds like bad news."

"It is for Mr. Nathanael, but good for us because the perpetrator has made his methods and signature more obvious—which means he's also exposed himself. It should allow us to identify him."

"And the bad news?" Clara braced herself. If the good news was bad, how awful was the bad news going to be?

"We may not have much time. He's obviously getting desperate. And…"

"And what?" *Here it comes.*

"And young Mr. Nathanael's struggling, Miss Clara. His subconscious is fighting very hard against whoever this is, but he's losing the ability to differentiate between his feelings in dreams and in real life."

"So his feelings for this woman, whoever she is, are becoming real?" *He doesn't really love her.* Sympathy for Nate warred with giddiness, swiftly replaced by disgust at herself. *Nate's in trouble and all you're worried about is yourself.*

"To him, yes. The negative emotions he's feeling—the suffocation, the fear when he looks at her—that's him trying to fight back. It's remarkable, really, his strength of will. Unfortunately, it might also be his undoing."

"What do you mean?" Surely if Nate's will was so strong, he'd be able to overcome this.

"Well, the more he fights back, the more pressure the manipulator will apply, either until Nate complies or—"

"Or he fries his brain."

"Right. And Nathanael becomes trapped in his own nightmares."

Tears welled in Clara's eyes. Poor Nate. He'd been fighting all this time, and she'd thought the worst of him. She'd been so selfish, thinking only how his dreams related to her and made her feel, never once wondering what they meant to him beyond the clinical interpretation.

"Miss Clara?" Ari laid a kind hand on Clara's arm. "I know how you feel about Mr. Nathanael, and—"

"You do?" Embarrassment warmed her skin. Clara had always thought she'd hidden it well, *especially* from her colleagues. It was undignified. Who else knew?

Ari seemed to read her mind. "Don't worry, my dear. It's nothing you've done. It's just the way things are meant to be. I've known both of you your entire lives, and you were made for each other. I know you know it, and Mr. Nathanael does as well."

"He does?" It was ridiculous to expect this woman to reassure her about her love life at a time like this, but Clara couldn't help it. Like Ari had said, she'd known them both all their lives.

"Of course. One only has to see him look at you to know there's no one else for him." Her smile creased her entire face.

Who would have thought old Ari would turn out to be such a romantic? "But the way he feels about me in his dreams…"

"The manipulation, nothing more."

"Even the good feelings?"

"No." Ari's eyes crinkled at the corners as she smiled. "Those are real, I'm sure of it."

I'll have to take her word for it. "And the other women, his teasing—"

"Why is it that exceptional young women never seem to recognize their own worth? Miss Clara, I mean no disrespect when I say this to you, but up until now, I thought you were too good for Mr. Nathanael." She held up her hand as Clara's mouth dropped open. "Let me finish. He has a kind heart, but he's flighty, irresponsible, and completely unaware of his own privilege. Until today, I'd have considered him beneath you, and I believe he's smart enough to feel it too. His behavior merely reflects that."

Could it be true? That Nate felt the same way but thought she was too good for him? It just seemed so trite, and so unlike him. "What do you mean, before today?"

"After seeing how hard he's trying to resist something so insidious…well, he must love you a great deal, more than I ever would've given him credit for."

Nate loved her. Really loved her. The way she wanted. She still didn't quite believe it, but any hope in the face of the last few weeks of despair was enough. "So what do we do? Can we help him?"

"Yes. We must find out who's behind this and why they're doing it. I think I may have a lead on the who, but I'll need a bit of time to confirm it. We have to be very careful about this, Miss Clara. We can't let anyone know what we're doing, in case we tip off whoever's behind this." Ari's mouth pinched as though she'd tasted something foul. "Whoever they are, they're good—and dangerous. They may decide to harm Mr. Nathanael if they think they're close to being found out."

So much for that emergency flight to Draglight. "What about Loth?"

"I know you'll tell him even if I tell you not to, so yes. If you think you can trust him."

"Of course I can." Loth was her *twin*, for goodness' sake.

"Mmm." Ari's mouth was a thin line. "We also need to figure out the how and the why."

"Okay, I—" Clara's transcomm gave a shrill squawk, and she glanced down to check the message.

Hi Clara. This is Siegmund, one of Nate's friends at uni. We need to talk.

Clara showed the message to Ari. "I think I might have a lead myself."

THIRTEEN

Three days. It had been three days since Nate had gazed upon his obsession's face, and he was going to die of hunger. Where had she gone, his dear Olympia? Everywhere he went, he was plagued by visions of her. The shimmering blue of her eyes in the iridescent feathers of the peacocks roaming the school grounds, the burnished auburn of her hair in the bottom of his wine glass. He'd even stared at her image in the university lake for hours, until he realized it was his own reflection.

He was going to break down Spalazani's front door and demand to see her if he hadn't laid eyes on her by the end of the day. Otherwise, he would starve.

His mind made up, Nate prepared what he would say to his professor, how to best plead his case before resorting to violence. Spalazani guarded his daughter jealously, and Nate, given the lack of attention he paid in class, was not, at present, one of his favorite pupils.

A commotion outside his window startled him to his feet. Had Olympia returned? He glanced down at himself, tugging at the hem of his vest and flicking away invisible dirt. A flash of regret shot through him that he didn't have time to properly groom himself, but love didn't wait.

Only it wasn't love arriving at Spalazani's front door, it was a catering company.

Sieg stood outside his and Nate's house, watching the activity with an amused expression. Nate hurried over to him. What could be going on? It wasn't a holiday or any other special occasion, as far as he knew.

Sieg answered before Nate could even ask. "Looks like old Spala's having a party."

"What kind of party?" Nate tried to keep his voice level, though heat had crept up his throat and burned behind his eyes. If he was invited, he'd get to see Olympia again.

"It's a debutante ball for that strange daughter of his. We're all invited. *And* it's tonight."

Tonight? "Why so sudden?" Balls usually took weeks to arrange.

"No idea. But hey, who are we to question a party?" He slung his arm over Nate's shoulder. "Come on, let's go get ready."

Yes. Nate had to make himself look his best for Olympia. He stared at his closet in dismay. Nothing he owned seemed quite right, all too young, too casual for the debut of such a fine woman. He finally settled on a midnight-black tuxedo. Where had he gotten it? Ah yes, from his best friend's sister, Clara. She was a nice girl. He'd cared for her once, a childish crush.

He gazed at himself in the mirror. Yes, that would do nicely. He looked elegant enough to ask even as refined a woman as Olympia for a dance. Satisfied, he practiced a few steps while watching his reflection. Thank goodness he could hold his own on the dance floor. Clara had taught him...

Clara.

I love Clara.

He'd always loved her. He'd danced with her at *her* debutante ball. She'd hated every minute of it, and he'd been secretly glad when she'd escaped with him and Loth to the terrace. There'd been too many other accomplished young men there, hoping to catch her eye. She'd looked so beautiful, like—

"Looking good, Nate. I might even ask you for a dance or two." Sieg lounged in the hallway outside Nate's room, rakish in a cobalt blue tuxedo and artfully undone bowtie. "Are you ready to go?"

What had he been thinking about? It seemed important. But Sieg was already hurrying away down the hall. Never mind. He would think of it later, after the party. With a tingle of anticipation, he closed the door behind him and sprinted after his housemate.

Yes, tonight was going to be a dream.

***

Considering the ball had been put together on such short notice, Spalazani's house was full of guests, and the normally austere house so blazing with lights and drenched with golden decorations that it almost hurt Nate's eyes.

But none of the grandeur could compare to that of the ball's shining star. Olympia sat on a mock throne at one end of the room, gazing serenely out over the heads of her courtiers. She was resplendent in white, like a bride, the slightly old-fashioned dress overlaid with golden lace. It had a high neck, sleeves covered the length of her arms down to her hands, and the skirts were so full, they clustered around her legs like the petals on a rose.

An urge crept over Nate to drop to his knees right there and then and beg for her just to *look* at him, to acknowledge him in some way. And he probably would've done just that, had Sieg not pushed a drink into his hand and steered him away. The moment she was out of his sight, his enthusiasm cooled, but only a fraction. Still, he was able to spend the next hour in polite conversation with the other guests and steal only the occasional glance at the stunning figure at the head of the room. As her guests enjoyed cocktail after cocktail, Olympia sat motionless, her expression composed and regal. The attendees tossed around murmured words like *snobbish* and *stuck up, cold* and *haughty*, but to be the center of attention at such a large gathering and remain so unruffled? She really was remarkable. Nate could think of only one other woman so self-possessed.

Clara.

Confusion wreathed his brain like fog.

Clara. Olympia. Clara.

A hand tugged at his arm, rousing him. What had he been thinking about?

"Come on, Nate. It's time to go to the recital room and hear the obligatory concert." Sieg had managed to steal a tray from one of the waiters and loaded it down with as many drinks as it could carry. "If you can stay awake, I'll even share my drinks with you."

Nate followed him to the next room. The program among the debuts of Foxwept's elite was always the same. First, the cocktail hour then the debutante's recital where she would perform for the audience. Loth's sister, Clara, had simply sat at the front of the room and glared at everyone for an hour. He and Loth had been in stitches at the audience's palpable discomfort, but as she was both the debutante and her own sponsor, there was nothing the audience could do but sit for the full hour and applaud politely at the end.

Clara.

A hush fell over the room as Olympia took her place stiffly on a dais before the audience. She struck up the first chord on the piano and as she opened her mouth, her voice transcended any human sound, lifting Nate from his seat and transporting him to the heavens. Through the clouds he soared with her, rising and falling with the notes, swelling with the final crescendo until his heart threatened to burst with feeling, an exquisite self-destruction he would've embraced with ecstasy.

The rest of the audience fell away, and Olympia played for him alone. Their eyes locked and as her fingers moved deftly over the keys, so they did over his spine, until, with the dying of the final note, Nate leaped to his feet, bringing his hands together in frenetic applause and shouting "Bravo! Bravo!" into the uninterested silence.

That got the audience to react, and they burst into a thunder of laughter.

Nate glanced around at them, all seated and dignified but himself, and his cheeks burned. How could they not be moved by her voice? Obviously, her performance had been too cultured for their vulgar tastes. They probably would've preferred a striptease. Rage built in him, a blind, hot anger that they should be so disrespectful. Well, he would tell them exactly what he thought about that.

He was saved from further embarrassment by Professor Spalazani, who materialized at the front of the room and offered Olympia his hand to rise from the piano and take her bow. The audience applauded then, so loudly and enthusiastically that the first words of Nate's diatribe were drowned out, and his thirst for their approval sated.

He retreated to the wall to watch as members of the audience filed up to the stage and congratulated the young songstress. He could wait his turn. Soon the dancing would begin, and that was when he would make his move, screwing up his courage and asking her to be his partner. Did he dare? Would she say yes? If she didn't, would he die right there on the spot? Or would his disappointment strangle him slowly in the night, as she, his puppeteer, tightened her strings around his neck?

Just as Nate could no longer stand the suspense, the first strains of orchestral music rose from the ballroom and there was a great rustling of skirts as the guests followed their host through the grand arches. Nate pushed his way through, not caring whose foot he crushed, or how much over-exposed cleavage he had to elbow past.

His perseverance paid off, and he was the first young man to stand in front of the glorious debutante. She stood, still cool and composed, none of the exertion of having just given an hour-long concert visible on her exquisite face.

He bowed low before her. "Dear Olympia, would you please do me the great honor of allowing me to escort you for this dance?" He held his breath, his entire existence dependent on her answer.

She said nothing but raised her hand to accept his.

Nate's heart swelled with joy. She had deigned to dance with him!

Olympia was a woman of contradictions. She'd sung so warmly, but her hand was cold and stiff in his own. Her nerves were understandable, however, and the chill of her skin didn't bother Nate.

I'll soon warm her up.

As he spun her around, the glittering room passed in a blur of lights and laughter, of flashes of every color under the sun. Sure enough, Olympia's hand soon warmed in his, and she gazed at him with such love and longing that it became his heart's greatest wish to have her as his partner for the rest of the night. Surely, looking at him the way she did, she didn't want a different partner?

And for Nate, the stars seemed to align. Under Nate's withering gaze, only a few other men approached Olympia that night, and those who did soon decided it wasn't worth the trouble. Indeed, the only time Nate was forced from her side was when she stepped out for the obligatory dance with her father, the professor. For the rest of the evening, she was Nate's alone.

Like most young men of his pedigree, Nate had learned to dance at an early age and considered himself quite proficient at it. Next to Olympia's perfectly timed and executed steps, however, he bumbled like a fool. Not once did she miss a step or fall out of time, but turned and stepped with a clockwork precision, often leaving Nate rushing to catch up.

His clumsiness seemed to be a source of great amusement, if the whispers and titters of the crowd were any indication. Or, more likely, it was the resentful laughter of the jealous. Well, they could laugh all they wanted. He distracted Olympia as best he could, whispering little jokes and compliments, and describing all the wonderful places he could take her, if she only she'd let him.

But still, the cruel behavior of the crowd must've gotten to her, for she didn't speak the entire time they danced, merely sighing as she stared deep into Nate's soul. Round and round they danced, stopping only when the orchestra took a short break. As they sat, watching the crowd milling around the buffet table, Nate professed his feelings to her.

"Olympia, I understand that we barely know each other, but you're not like any woman I've ever met. And it sounds crazy, but I think I adore you." He held his breath. She didn't smile, but instead sighed and looked away.

She's so modest.

Most women would've giggled coquettishly and given a smug toss of their heads.

Yet another thing to admire about her. Then she gazed back at him, and within her eyes was a wisdom and depth of emotion so profound, it took his breath away.

Professor Spalazani passed them once or twice with a contented grin. And why wouldn't he be happy? Nate was wealthy, from a good family, and with unlimited prospects. He was more than a match for a professor's daughter. And even if Spalazani did discover a fault with him, Nate would overcome it.

When the orchestra fired up again, Nate led Olympia out on the dance floor and they twirled, faster and faster as the crowd, the room, the music blended together until, eventually, everything but Olympia's face ceased to exist. Had he ever been so happy before?

But exhausted at last, Nate had to admit he could no longer dance. They stopped, Nate gasping for breath and grinning as sweat poured down his face. Olympia, on the other hand, remained as cool as ever, with not a hair out of place.

The ballroom was empty. No soul remained but Olympia's father, who watched the couple from one of the empty tables. When had the people, the orchestra gone? Neither he nor Olympia had noticed when the music and the laughter fell silent.

All we saw was each other.

And now came the moment Nate had dreaded the entire night—it was time to leave Olympia and go home. Disentangling his hands from hers brought an almost physical pain, as though he were tearing off a layer of his own skin. As she and Spalazani walked him to the front door, he had to know.

"Olympia, do you love me?" As he gazed deep into her eyes, his heart seemed to pause as it waited for her answer.

She didn't speak, but sighed, as she'd done the rest of the evening.

It didn't matter. He understood her well enough by now to know her answer was yes. So, as Spalazani looked on approvingly, Nate leaned over and kissed her.

He was met by a shocking chill. Her lips were like ice, and a shiver of revulsion passed over him. He pushed it quickly away. Of course she was going to be cold after expending all her energy dancing. She was probably exhausted.

And she had nothing to eat or drink. Guilt lashed at him. *It's my fault. I can't believe I was so thoughtless.*

"A good night's sleep will soon bring the warmth back to those lips," he said fondly to her, and she sighed again then turned and left the room. He was watching her go, admiring the curve of her waist, when Spalazani laid a hand on his shoulder.

"I'm pleased to see you and Olympia getting along so well, Nathanael."

"She is a remarkable woman." Nate's gaze lingered on the doorway through which she'd gone.

"Indeed she is. You're welcome to come and visit whenever you like, Nathanael. Olympia doesn't have many friends, so I think she'd really like the company."

If Nate had suddenly grown wings, his spirits couldn't have been higher. Only one night, and her father had already given Nate his stamp of approval. Better to quit now, before he said something stupid and ruined it.

"Thank you, sir, I'll do that." He bowed deeply to Spalazani and left, his feet barely touching the ground as he made his way home.

FOURTEEN

The face staring back at Loth and Clara was handsome in that blond, blue-eyed, chiseled, rich-boy way.

So this is the infamous Sieg.

Whenever Nate was led astray, Sieg always seemed to be involved somehow. Clara had never met him, and given his reputation for hedonism, she'd had no desire to. The fact that *he* was calling her, presumably about Nate, worried her. Maybe the situation was even worse than she'd thought.

"You must be Clara. I mean, Nate told me you were beautiful, but—"

Oh for goodness' sake. "Save your charm for someone who cares, Sieg." Why did these men always assume flattering women about their looks was the best way to start a conversation? Did they truly think all women were that vain and easily sweet-talked?

His smile fell. "Sorry. Old habit. Even if it is true."

Clara rubbed the headache beginning between her eyes. "Why are you calling me? I'm sorry to be abrupt, but I—"

"I think Nate's in trouble, Clara. I didn't know who else to talk to." He'd dropped the playboy act and was looking openly concerned.

That couldn't be good, if a playboy like Sieg was worried about Nate's behavior. "Why? What's happened?"

"When was the last time you spoke to Nate?"

"He sent me a message the other week...but since then, nothing. His message seemed normal enough. I tried to contact him but had no reply. I assumed he was studying for exams."

Sieg frowned. "Nate? Studying?"

"Hey, he does—" Loth leaned forward and glared at the screen.

"Sorry, I didn't mean that to be offensive." Sieg shrugged apologetically.

"It wasn't." Clara turned to Loth. "Look, we both love Nate, but let's be honest, academics isn't his strong point. And," she added as her brother began to protest, "there's nothing wrong with that. Can we please just get to the point?"

"Fine. Go ahead." But Loth remained on the defensive, his brow creased in warning.

Sieg hesitated. "Before I tell you everything that's happened in the last few days, Clara, I have to ask— Have you and Nate had a fight?"

"A little one, when he was home. But we patched things up. Why?"

"Oh hell. This is so awkward. I...I don't really know how to say this because I know you and he..." Sieg's eyes darted back and forth as though he didn't know where to look. "But—"

"He's in love with another woman." *Clara* could say it. She didn't want to hear anyone else say it, though—that would make it real.

Sieg visibly relaxed. "Yes. You knew?"

"I had an inkling." Should she tell Sieg about Nate's dreams? *No.* The fewer people who knew, the better. Sieg, despite his best intentions, might let something slip about someone messing with Nate's dreams to the wrong person.

But Clara could still use his help. "I don't know any of the details. Could you please tell me everything you know?" She braced herself. Knowing Nate was being manipulated wasn't going to make hearing about it any less painful.

"Are you sure?"

Clara had never seen someone look so uncomfortable. Sieg may have had a reputation as a self-indulgent degenerate, but he did seem genuinely concerned for both of them. She softened. A bit.

"Yes, please. It's important." She glanced over at Loth, who nodded. "We think something's wrong with him, Sieg, so any information you have, no matter how hurtful you think it might be, would be helpful."

Sieg ran his hand through his hair. "What exactly do you want me to tell you?"

"First off, who is she, this woman he's in love with?" Clara nearly vibrated with anticipation. If they could discover her identity, it might lead them to another clue.

"Her name's Olympia. She's the daughter of one of our professors."

Olympia. The woman Nate had told her about. *She looks like an angel, Clara… Forget her. I have.*

When Nate had told her about Olympia the first time, Clara had been uneasy. She should've trusted her instincts. *But even if you had, what would you have done about it? Forbidden him from going back to university? This isn't your fault, Clara.*

"Do you have a picture of her, by any chance?" She was pretty sure Olympia was the woman she was looking for, but she had to be certain. Her and Nate's future depended on it.

"Clara." Loth leaned forward from the couch. "You don't have to—"

"Yes, I do. It's important, Loth. You *know* that." She gave him a look. She'd told him about Nate's dreams, and about her and Ari's preliminary findings. He hadn't been sure what to make of them, and Clara suspected he didn't really believe any of it. "Please, Sieg?"

"I should have a picture from the ball. Just give me a second." He disappeared momentarily from the screen.

"Ball?" Loth asked. "Nate went to a *ball*? Willingly?"

"It was Olympia's debutante ball." Sieg was back. "It was...interesting. But I'll get back to that in a minute." He held up his transcomm. "Here, the woman in the gold and white. That's her."

It was the woman from Nate's dream.

She was real. Clara swallowed hard around a sudden lump in her throat. "And she's the daughter of one of your professors?"

"Yes, Professor Spalazani."

Clara noted that down. It was a possible lead. She'd have to look into this professor. "So tell us about the ball."

"Well, Nate changed even before the ball. He...he suddenly became infatuated with Olympia. He'd spend hours staring out his window at her—he probably told you our dorm burnt down, and we moved into a house just across the street from Spalazani's."

Nate had told them about the fire, but *not* about his new neighbors.

"It got to the point that all he talked about was her. It was like he was becoming obsessed."

"*Like* he was becoming obsessed?" Loth scoffed. "If Nate does anything consistently for more than an hour, he *has* to be obsessed." Clara was surprised by the edge to his voice. Nate could usually do no wrong in his eyes—he'd been defending him only moments ago. But after what had happened on the terrace...was Loth losing faith in him?

"Maybe, but that was nothing like what happened at the ball." And Sieg proceeded to tell them everything—Nate's wild applause and overzealous praise, the possessiveness with which he'd held the debutante the entire evening, the way she was still in his arms as Sieg, one of the last of the guests to leave, finally gave up and went home.

"I...I heard him telling her he...adored her." He winced. "Oh, Clara, I'm so sorry."

Clara had to turn away for a few moments. Every word Sieg spoke was a cut to her heart. Even if they made it through this, the wound was so deep it might never heal.

But when she turned back, she kept her expression stoic. *I will see this through, no matter how much it hurts. This isn't Nate. Remember that. He's being controlled.*

"The thing is, I just don't understand his attraction to her. I can't imagine anyone being interested in her for more than a few minutes, never mind being *obsessed* with her."

"She's a beautiful woman." It stung, but it was true. Olympia had the kind of face history went to war over.

"Yes, but so what? It's not like Nate doesn't have a million gorgeous women interested in him." Sieg blushed as though he'd just remembered who he was talking to. "Um, besides, she's not that beautiful, not once you get to know her."

"What do you mean?"

"She's just so unlike what I thought he wanted."

"What, beautiful, cultured, and living next door?"

"No, Clara, *you*. Nate talks about you all the time. Until the last couple of weeks, I thought he was obsessed with *you*." He leaned closer to the screen, as though to add weight to his words. "Don't let those other women fool you. Nate can be an idiot about these things, but his heart knows what it wants." Sieg looked faintly embarrassed. "But this Olympia…she's so stiff and cold, expressionless. She never smiles, never speaks." He frowned. "I don't know if there's something wrong with her, or if she just thinks she's better than everyone else. She almost doesn't seem human. I've heard people calling her a wax-face, a wooden doll…so it isn't just me who sees her this way. It's *everyone*, apart from Nate. That's what makes it so strange."

"Do you see much of her?"

"Not really, no. Spala pretty much keeps her a secret. Maybe because of the way she is? I just don't know. Does she have some kind of medical problem?" Sieg shook himself. "Sorry. I just…I just don't get it."

"Have you talked to Nate about it at all? I know he considers you a good friend."

"I tried the day after the ball. A few of us did. We pointed out her behavior to him… Maybe it was the way I went about it, but I thought he was going to murder me. He even went so far as to say he would, if I ever showed an interest in her."

Clara pressed her fingers to her throat. Nate had *never* been violent, nor even threatened it. *Unless you count that day on the terrace.* She pushed the thought away. It just wasn't the Nate she knew.

"I told him about the gossip—that she was beautiful but soulless, as though she were a robot, that people were joking that she *is* a robot. That she's too perfect. I mean, you should've seen her performance at the ball. Not a single stray note, flawless timing…people just don't play like that. It's not natural."

Could it be true? Could Olympia be an android? "You mean like a synadroid?" Sentient androids had recently been emancipated and were integrating themselves more visibly in Foxwept.

"A synadroid? Hell, no. I can barely tell them apart from humans. They *have* emotions. This Olympia…when I say robot, I mean *robot*. Like an automaton."

"That sounds…pretty damn unnerving." *And not possible*. Nate could be blind to things right in front of him at times, but mistaking a lifeless robot for a real woman? Could the manipulation be that complete?

"Honestly, some of us are genuinely scared of her, and of what might happen to Nate. But Spala seems bent on encouraging him—and who could blame him? Nate's a catch."

If this Spalazani was encouraging the relationship, she couldn't be a robot…but what was it then?

"What did Nate say about all that? I assume he wasn't pleased."

"You're damn right he wasn't. At first, he was really angry, but then he calmed down and defended her rationally, saying other people simply couldn't appreciate her, that they were jealous, that she understood all the higher principles of life, whatever *that* means. He said I was too ignorant to understand."

He defended her rationally. That was the most worrying.

"But then, you know, we also had a bit of a moment where he seemed to understand that I was trying to help him, and he didn't fight me after that. That seemed worse, somehow." He scrubbed his hands over his face. "Anyway, I just wanted you to know. I'm worried, Clara, and I figured you would be as well. I...I just don't know what to do."

Clara chewed her lip as her mind raced. "Leave it with me, Sieg. I have a few ideas. But can you do me a favor? It will help Nate."

"For Nate? Count me in." He sat straighter in his chair.

"Can you find out anything you can about this Spalazani, please? And Olympia? The more information we have, the easier it'll be to figure out what's going on and how we can help Nate."

"Ugh." Sieg's shoulders slumped. "I was hoping to stay away from that house as much as possible. But if it'll help Nate, I'll do it. I can also keep an eye on him."

"Thank you so much, Sieg. You're a good friend."

Sieg blushed. "That's kind of you to say, Clara, especially because I know what you must think of me. And I don't blame you," he added hurriedly.

"Take care, and let me know what you find out."

"I will, and you do too. We'll get Nate back, I promise." The screen went black.

"Okay. This is great, Loth. Olympia is the woman from Nate's dreams. So we just need to find the connection between her and whoever's manipulating Nate." She spun to look at her brother.

She'd never seen such an expression of rage on Loth's face before. She hadn't thought it possible for him to *be* that angry. "Loth? What's wrong?"

"What's wrong? Nate! Nate's what's wrong."

"Yes, but he's being manipulated and—"

"Oh, wake up, Clara! How can such a smart woman be so stupid?"

Clara blinked at him. Where was this coming from? "I don't—"

"I know how you feel about him, Clara. How you *really* feel."

Though they talked about everything else, this was a subject they'd always danced around. But she wasn't surprised.

"He's being manipulated? No, Clara, he's doing what he always does—taking you for granted and treating you like crap—and you're making excuses for him."

"No, Loth. This time—"

"This time! This time he's *in love with someone else* and hasn't even had the decency to tell you. I've always stood up for Nate because I thought that deep down, he was in love with you, Clara. That he always has been." He got up and started pacing. "All those flings…they meant nothing. Sure, they were stupid and inappropriate, and there were times I wanted to punch him in the face because I know they hurt you, the same way your relationships with other men hurt him." He shook his head. "But I looked the other way because I truly believed the two of you would end up together. Now…I'm done with him, Clara. I detest him for treating you like this—and I detest you for letting him."

"But he isn't in control of his own actions!"

Loth's hands clenched at his sides. "He's publicly declaring his love for her! He's humiliating you. You need to forget him."

"Loth, please. Don't give up on him—or me—just yet. We're so close to finding out what's behind this,

I'm sure of it. Before you write him off, just give us more time. You've been best friends since you were babies. Don't throw it away."

Loth's mouth twisted as he looked down at his hands. "Clara—"

"Please." She dropped to her knees in front of him. "Please, Loth. For me. I promise you, if I find out that Nate's doing all this under his own steam, I'll have nothing more to do with him." She pressed her cheek to his leg.

He stroked his hand over her hair, and when she glanced up, his expression was sad. "Do you mean that, Clara? If he turns out to be the bastard he seems to be, you'll kick him to the curb?"

"I promise." And she would. She loved Nate, and she always would. But she loved herself, and her own heart, even more. It was how she'd made it this far and kept her sanity, the only way she'd be able to face whatever was happening head-on.

Loth exhaled heavily. "Fine. I'll keep my peace for now. But," he held up a hand as Clara smiled, "I *am* going to find out the legal and financial ramifications if we end up needing to split the company."

When had he gotten so responsible? Clara didn't like even the thought of splitting up Dreaming Life, but she could live with it. It would buy her the time she needed, at any rate.

"Thank you, Loth. I love you."

"Whatever. Get up off the damn floor."

She rose into his embrace. It had been a long time since they'd hugged each other, and she'd forgotten how good it felt. Loth was her only living family, and whatever happened with Nate, they had to stay strong. Stay together. If they could do that, they'd survive.

"So what next?"

"I'm going to go tell Ari what I've found and see if it matches up with any of her information." She raised an eyebrow as Loth recoiled. "You don't give her enough credit, you know. She's actually pretty wonderful once you get to know her."

"I'll take your word for it." He stood and stretched. "Right, well while you're off playing detective, I've got a company to run."

Just after Loth closed the door behind him, the alert on Clara's terminal sounded.

A dream.

FIFTEEN

Clara was at another wedding. And this time, it was her own. Or, more accurately, her and Nate's. But it wasn't their first wedding. The off-kilter placard above the doorway proclaimed that today was their 101st anniversary, and they were renewing their vows.

But rather than the pride of accomplishment filling Nate's chest, the sign provoked a gut-wrenching nausea. 101 years? How was that possible? Unless...they were in a Dreaming Life simulation. Yes. That was it. Clara wouldn't let him die. She kept their bodies alive, year after year, entwined in their shared bed, never to die, never to live again.

Clara gagged as vomit rose in Nate's throat then ground her teeth together so hard the enamel threatened to shatter. He would not give Clara the satisfaction of seeing the misery his marriage to her had wrought. A vise seized his hand, a hold so strong his bones bowed and crumbled within his flesh. It was Clara, baring her teeth up at him as she used the death grip to pull him along, yet again, toward hell.

Nate and Clara's dream doppelgangers made their way to the altar, his steps faltering, unsteady. Hers were victorious, dragging his frail body along like prey. They stood at the altar, inhaling the scent of mildew and waiting for the ceremony to begin. Nates knees began to fail and yet Clara forced him to stand, to bear witness as she punished him yet again.

The weathered benches of the hall were empty, but as the miasma of rot grew stronger, guests filed in, gliding over the cracked stone floor and dressed in the black of mourning. It was time for the ceremony binding Nate to Clara for an eternity to begin.

She peered at her bride. Dream-Clara was also dressed in black, and her features were oddly irregular, as though someone had either created her from a befuddled memory or with an intentional unkindness. She stared at Nate with an expression so depraved, so delighted with the anguish she brought him that acid again burned the back of his throat. Perhaps if his tongue dissolved, she would grow tired of his silence and let him die. He welcomed the pain.

The bile grew thicker as Nate recognized some of the guests. His father was there, his face ruined by the explosion that had taken his life, his clothes singed and marred by soot. He gazed at the couple morosely, muttering with his ruined mouth. Nate ached to throw himself at his father's feet, to beg for the comfort of his childhood, to be a boy, safe from the woman Clara had become. If only he could change places with his father, he could find peace as ashes, too fine for her to hold in her grasp.

Clara's father was there too, and she resisted the urge to run to his side and throw her arms around him. His face was gaunt, his mouth turned down as it seldom had in life. The mark of his death was on him, a purple bruise that covered his chest, visible under his open collar. Clara's mother twisted her hands around one of the lace handkerchiefs she'd always carried, her head tucked under her arm, the stump of her neck cauterized by the red-hot steel that had killed her.

"Why did he marry her?" Nate's father's voice reached them at last. "How could this happen?" His voice was slurred, charred flesh flaking from his lips.

"It was my fault," her father wheezed around his collapsed lungs. "I made them promise. But I was wrong." He shook his head. "So very wrong." Her mother's head could only weep, the tears running down her arm and staining the lace.

As the melancholy priest, his robes blooming with decay, bound them in marriage, the guests lamented and pulled at their hair, their voices rising in a dirge that eventually drowned out the couple's vows. Nate raised his hands to his face as dream-Clara gazed at him, and Clara recoiled. His skin was old, so old and worn. It wasn't the face of a man who'd married the love of his life, but rather a man who'd been sentenced to death, condemned to the cell of his life with a front-row view of the gallows.

As the ceremony finally came to an end, Nate and dream-Clara faced their guests.

"And now," announced Nate, "we shall take refreshments on the—"

Dream-Clara put her hand on his arm. "Our guests shall take refreshments, but not us. No, we shall live on love alone."

Nate was starving.

Hunger gnawed at him, a deep and agonizing emptiness that despaired of ever being filled. It consumed him from the inside, leaching the life from him, and as he gazed at his bride, he wished it would hurry up and kill him. Not that she would let it.

First was the honeymoon.

"Where will you go? Will you go abroad?" The guests appeared hopeful, as though they wished them far, far away.

Nate desperately wanted to go somewhere he had no other memories of. Perhaps, if they went far enough away, he could become someone else. Or Clara could. Or perhaps they could rediscover each other, and he would remember why, after all these years of wretchedness, he'd married her in the first place.

"We won't be going anywhere." Dream-Clara sucked air over her synthetic teeth. "Why would we, when everything we need is right here, with each other?" She ground the bones of his hands together again. "At least, for the next hundred years."

Nate, unable to stand any more, dropped to his knees in front of all their guests, and pleaded for death to come and swallow him at last.

Clara's visor was slick with tears as she struggled to claw it from her face. Even once it was off, she couldn't shake Nate's prayers from her ears. She rose from her desk and stood before the expansive window, pressing her fingertips to the glass.

This isn't him. This isn't him. She closed her eyes. *Not yet, anyway.*

But one thing was clear—Nate was losing to whomever was doing this. And Clara was losing him.

***

"I've never seen anything so cruel," Ari murmured.

Arienne had been on the other side of Clara's office door when she'd opened it, poised to fly down the hall to the older woman's laboratory. She'd

134

stared wordlessly at Ari then collapsed into her arms, sobbing.

"They're definitely getting worse." Clara dropped her head in her hands. "We need to find out who's behind this."

"I think I know who it is, Miss Clara. That's what I came to tell you."

"Who is it?"

"Does the name Coppelius mean anything to you?"

The floor shifted beneath Clara's feet. *Coppelius. The Sandman.* She struggled to find her voice. "Yes. Nate told me about him. And his suspicions about Coppelius's involvement in his father's death."

Ari's face darkened. "Yes. I've always had questions about that myself. I knew that horrid man back in the day, and I wouldn't put cold-blooded murder past him."

"You *knew* him?"

"Unfortunately, yes. That's how I was able to recognize his signature. Arrogant ass. He could've covered his tracks perfectly, but he's always been a narcissist and couldn't help but leave a marker of his identity behind."

"This is great news! Now we just have to find him."

"That might be a bigger problem than you think, Miss Clara."

"Why? Ari, you know the resources we have. If he's anywhere in the Blackmoth Republic, we'll find him."

"He's dead, Miss Clara. Or supposed to be. That's why it took me so long to identify him. I thought it simply wasn't possible."

"Dead? But then—"

"He's obviously not. He must've faked his death. Or else he's the devil, which wouldn't surprise me. What I don't understand is what he would want with Mr. Nathanael."

"I think it might have something to do with his father." Clara recounted what Nate had told her about that night he'd been caught spying. "But he couldn't be holding a grudge against him for *that*, could he?"

"I wouldn't put that past him either. The man was a viper. But there has to be more to it than that. Much more." Her shoulders stiffened. "Wait. You said Mr. Nathanael was rendered color-blind when he was a child?"

"Yes. When he was ten. It was right after—" Realization prickled her skin. "Right after the incident with Coppelius."

Ari slapped her hand on Clara's desk. "That's it, then. *That's* how's he doing it." Her smile was wide, and color tinted her cheeks. Victory looked good on her.

"I thought you said the color chip wasn't powerful enough to support these manipulations?"

"In those early days, when Nathanael's father and Coppelius were still working together, they were testing numerous prototypes. Used to carry around eyeballs in a case." She shuddered. "I never did know where they got them. Anyway, one of the main issues they had with the early VR prototypes was that they caused color-blindness within the simulation, and, rarely, it made the patients color-blind as well. It was a big problem, of course, because not only would the therapeutic reality be unbelievable, but Nate's father refused to put their patients at risk. It took them months to overcome it, if I recall correctly."

"So you think they implanted a chip in Nate that night?" The thought of it left her cold.

"It would explain why it was so traumatic for him, and why he took ill afterward. His body was reacting to the chip. The color blindness is too much of a coincidence."

Clara had to agree. But still. "I can't believe his father—"

"Don't be too hard on his father, Miss Clara. I mean, yes, it was his fault, and while part of me can't believe that Edward would do that to his own son...he was under a huge amount of pressure at the time. If they couldn't get the chips to work, they would lose all their shareholders' faith. And money. Dreaming Life would fail."

"But why put the chip in Nate?"

"It was unethical—and illegal—to use living subjects. Perhaps they believed that if it worked in Nathanael, the committee that oversaw these things would allow them to start live trials. They would've gotten their wrists slapped, of course, but that would've been nothing compared to how their success would've been received. Any duplicity on their part would've been swept under the proverbial rug."

"But it was a failure. Nate also became color-blind."

"Yes. It must've been a huge disappointment. Then only a year later, Edward was dead. I doubt it was a coincidence."

"Do you have any idea why Coppelius would've wanted to kill Nate's father? I mean, they did get the prototype working months before his death. Dreaming Life's success was assured."

Ari pulled on her lip. "I can't say for sure, although I did overhear them arguing in the laboratory once. Nathanael's father—and your parents, as well—wanted Dreaming Life to be what is now is, a treatment option for patients. Edward wanted it to be as cheap as possible for hospitals, even if they took a loss. He figured they could make up the financial difference in other ways, such as video games. But Coppelius had other ideas. He wanted to sell it to the military or the government. I thought it was for training purposes, combat situations and the like, but now..."

"He had other reasons."

"Yes. Imagine if the government or the military were able to manipulate our dreams? Or if it fell into the wrong hands? Hands that had unimaginable amounts of money?"

The two women stared at each other.

"Definitely worth killing over." Ari pressed her lips into a thin line.

"But he couldn't have done anything with the design. Nate's father had patented it with ironclad rights and already signed everything over to Nate's trust in the event of his death."

"But Coppelius wouldn't have known that. He might've thought that, as partner, all rights would revert to him. That project wasn't part of your father's remit, just Edward and Coppelius's."

So Coppelius had a motive. "But how would he get to Nate to initiate the transmission in the first place? Those chips don't have much range when dormant. Surely he'd have to get close to him to establish that first link." A terrible suspicion began to creep over her.

"It could've happened anywhere. He'd only have to be a few feet away. In a crowd, or a—"

"Dorm room." Vandran, the optics dealer. How had Clara been so stupid?

If someone knew the right person and had enough money, they could alter the way they looked. And Coppelius had been so brazen, knowing full well Nate might recognize him.

The bastard was mocking them.

And Nate had known all along. But Clara, thinking she knew best, had practically gaslighted him.

"Yes, for the initial manipulation. But Nate's mind seems to have overcome it at first. For the complete exploitation we're seeing, he would've had to reinitiate the transmission with a stronger signal. Did Nathanael mention seeing him again?"

"No. But that doesn't mean he didn't. We're...not really speaking much right now."

Ari's sympathetic expression was almost as painful as Nate's dream, and the urge to throw herself into the others woman's arms and bawl her eyes out was overpowering. But now wasn't the time to wallow.

Clara took a deep breath. "So how can we help Nate?"

"I'm not sure. Ideally, we'd remove the chip."

"Which means we'd have to convince Nate of what's going on." It wouldn't be so hard to persuade him of what Coppelius had done, but Clara dreaded telling him Edward had been involved. Nate still remembered his father with the heart of a child, and in his eyes, the man had died infallible. The thought that his father was complicit would be a far worse blow to Nate then the rest of it. But it had to be done.

"I'm afraid it's not that simple, Miss Clara."

"I don't think it'll be simple, Ari. I know it involves complex surgery, and—"

"It's not just that. We don't really know how Coppelius is transmitting those signals. If he finds out what we're doing, he might take action against Mr. Nathanael—and with a direct link to his brain, who knows what he'll do?"

"Can we not just block the signal? Or divert it somehow?"

"We could, but Coppelius would probably find his way around any blocks we put in place. It would be temporary, and once he reconnected, he might take swift revenge. No, removing the chip—all the chips—is the only way to be sure."

"So what do we do?"

"We have to find Coppelius, Miss Clara. Find him and make him stop, one way or another." She pursed her lips, but Clara understood. She would be willing to do anything to stop Coppelius. In the meantime, though, Nate was going to suffer.

"I—" Clara's voice swallowed itself, and tears threatened behind her eyes again.

Ari put her hand on Clara's shoulder. "Mr. Nathanael is strong, Miss Clara. We just have to give him whatever help we can. He'll do the rest."

Clara breathed slowly through the tightness in her throat. She would *not* cry. Not now. Maybe later, when it was all over. Right now, she had to think. "That leaves only one problem, then. Nate. What do we tell him?"

"What we know. Once we show him the logic of what—"

"The logic? Nate's not thinking logically right now, Arienne. He barely seems to remember who I am. Telling him that everything he feels and knows to be true right now is nothing more than a manipulation will crush him, as will his father's complicity. *If* he even believes us."

"Is there any way we could…get a medical order for him? Then at least he would be where you could keep an eye on him."

"You mean have him committed? He's not crazy, Ari."

"I know. But he's certainly acting out of character. It would be enough to convince the necessary authorities, and we could keep it discreet. No one outside of us and the medical staff would know, and they're legally sworn to secrecy."

"No. No way. I won't treat him like that. He was worried that's what we would think when he told Loth and me about Coppelius in the first place. I can't do that to him."

"There's no other way, Miss Clara. And we're running out of time."

"I'll think of something. Something to get him home." But then what? They had no idea how to stop Coppelius, even if Nate believed them. And why would he? Who would believe their own feelings were false? He didn't know he was being manipulated. And if she insisted, not only could it destroy their relationship, but Nate himself might start to think he was losing his mind. No way could she do that to him. No, Nate had to believe and accept what was happening to him. But how to get him to do that, she had no clue.

Clara often had her best ideas when she wasn't thinking about the problem at hand. *Focus on something else, and let your mind figure it out without you interfering.* It was how she solved her most difficult puzzles at work.

How do Professor Spalazani and Olympia play into what's happening? What's their connection to Coppelius? What could Coppelius possibly have to gain by making Nate fall in love with Olympia? "Do you know anyone called Spalazani?"

Ari tapped her finger on her chin. "No. I can't say I do."

"Oh." Deflated, Clara slumped down in her seat. "I guess that would've been too easy."

"Who is Spalazani? I mean, in the scheme of things?"

She rubbed her eyes. "He's a professor of Nate's. His daughter is the one from the dreams, the one Nate's obsessed with." She gave Ari a quick recap of the events of the ball.

Ari's brow creased so much she almost appeared to have eyebrows. "That...must've been very difficult for you to hear."

"It was." It *still* hurt, even now. "I just keep telling myself that it's not really Nate, that it's the Sandman—I mean, Coppelius."

"The Sandman?" Ari snorted. "I must say, that's very apt."

So what was the connection between Spalazani and Coppelius? She'd already searched the network for any information on Spalazani, but there didn't seem to be any news of note. In fact, other than a few articles announcing his tenure at Draglight, he didn't seem to exist until a few years ago.

But that was impossible. Unless...

What if Spalazani's not his real name? That has to be it. And there was one man who might be able to help her. *Sieg.* Clara sat straight in her chair and pulled up her messages. She typed quickly as she spoke to Ari over her shoulder. "I asked Nate's roommate to dig into Spalazani, but it never occurred to me that it might be a fake name." No wonder she'd heard nothing back.

Sieg, I don't think Spalazani is who he says he is. I need to you to find out his real name. I don't care how. Please, to help Nate. And keep an eye on them. All of them. Oh, also, do you have security footage outside your house? If so, send it to me.

Her message sent, Clara spun in her chair to face Ari. "Sieg is just as worried about Nate as we are. If there's anything to dig up about Spalazani, he'll do it."

Now what? Clara was a woman of action, and the questions buzzed around her mind like a swarm of bees, the answers infuriatingly out of reach. Who was Spalazani? Was he working with Coppelius? Why? And what role did Olympia play in all of it? Was she an accomplice? Or a victim?

"I'm going to drive myself crazy."

"I couldn't agree more, Miss Clara. You need to rest."

Ari was right. She needed sleep. Reluctantly, she rose. Perhaps she should just sleep here, in her office. If something came up, she would have everything she needed at her disposal.

"Goodnight, Miss Clara." And yet Ari stayed where she was, her teeth worrying her bottom lip.

"Ari? Is something wrong?" Whatever it was, Clara was ready to help. Ari had done so much for her.

The older woman smiled fondly. "No, Miss Clara. I just...I just wanted say thank you."

"Ari, *you're* the one who's been helping *me*. I should be saying thank you." *On my knees. Right now, you're the closest thing to a god I've got.*

"For...coming to me. Asking me for my help. *Trusting* me."

"But why wouldn't I? You've been here my whole life, and I—"

"I know how I seem to people. Like your brother, for example." She lifted a hairless brow. "I'm not the easiest person to get along with, nor work with. I often feel that the world is moving on without me. The day you first came to me with this, I was considering handing in my notice and retiring. But now you've given me a challenge." Her eyes flashed, and a smile curled her lips. "We're going to get this Coppelius, Miss Clara, and we're going to stop him. For what he's done."

Clara understood.

Ari wasn't helping her simply out of the goodness of her heart. She'd devoted her entire life to the dream constructs at Dreaming Life, and the perversion of her life's work by Coppelius was intolerable. A rush of affection surged through Clara. She understood this woman's heart all too well.

Impulsively, she yanked the drawer of her desk open and pulled out Loth's liquor. Sleep could wait. Tossing the cap aside, she took a long swig from the bottle then passed it to Ari with a toast.

"To stopping the Sandman."

SIXTEEN

"What do you think, my love?" Nathanael held his breath. For a moment, his heart seemed to stop beating, waiting to start again on Olympia's command. He'd just finished reciting another of his poems to her, this one exclusively about the striking vivacity of her eyes. It had run for over a hundred pages, and Nate considered it one of his greatest pieces to date.

"Although, I can't really take the credit for it. It was you who inspired me, Olympia. You're my muse. Everything I write is motivated by you." He stroked the notebook lovingly, as though it were an extension of her.

Olympia smiled and leaned closer to Nate, but didn't speak, though her eyes plainly showed that his words had touched the very depths of her soul. What a gift she was. Never had Nate's writing been more alive, flowed so easily. And it was all down to Olympia's careful consideration. Every time he read his work to her, she sat and listened, her gaze focused unwaveringly on his face. Not once did she twist her hands in her lap, or glance at the clock, or distract herself with anything but the sound of his voice. He'd never had such an attentive audience. He used to show Loth's sister Clara his work…

Clara.

He thought of her sometimes when waking, and an inexplicably deep sense of loss would grip his chest until he could barely breathe. And then the vestiges of sleep would clear, and Olympia was all he saw.

Olympia. The strength of her love was apparent in her silence. Whether at home with Nate reciting to her, or when walking along the Draglight shoreline, her ardent gaze remained fixed on him and her heart spoke instead. She never had to say a word, so completely in tune were they. The occasional sigh from her elegant lips was all the encouragement Nate needed.

And yet, it wasn't perfect. Sometimes, once Nate had returned to his room, there would be a break in the passionate fog of his mind. Siegmund was responsible for most of these interruptions.

"So what do you two talk about, anyway?" He lounged on Nate's bed as Nate hurried to complete their most recent assignment. It had been due yesterday, but Nate had obtained an extension from the professor by claiming illness then begged Sieg to walk him through it. To his surprise, Sieg, who loathed doing any more work than necessary, had readily agreed.

Nate shrugged, not taking his eyes off his screen. "I read stuff I've written to her, mostly."

"What? You mean, like business tax reform, or the future of exportation?"

Nate snorted. "Of course not. I read her...well, I read her poetry, that sort of thing."

"Poetry *you've* written?" Sieg's voice bubbled with mirth. "Really?"

"Yes. Why does that seem so strange. I...I wanted to be a writer and artist ever since I was little, Sieg."

"Then why are you here?"

"Because of…" *Why am I here, other than for Olympia?* "Dreaming Life. I can't run a business just building dreamscapes."

"But why work for Dreaming Life at all? You're independently wealthy, Nate. Why not just sell your shares and live the life you want?"

It took Nate a long time to find the answer. "Because at some point, it *was* the life I wanted. It was my father's legacy, after all." And there was something else, some other part of that life that he'd wanted more than anything. But what was it?

Ah yes, there'd been a girl, Clara. "I also had a crush on a girl, and Dreaming Life was her connection to me. As long as I was involved with the business, I was involved with her. That was a life I used to want."

"A *girl*? Do you mean—"

"Her name was Clara."

"Wait, *Clara*? Nate, Clara's not just a girl you had a crush on. Up until you met Olympia, Clara was the love of your life."

"Was she? Huh." He laughed. It sounded so melodramatic. "It seems so long ago, now. But like I said, it was just a crush."

"It was last *month*, Nate." Sieg shook his head.

"A lot can change in a month." But Sieg had a point. Why *was* he still here? He really had no reason to be at the university other than trying to uphold his father's legacy. And how important was legacy? Nate could create his own.

He was meant for something bigger than Dreaming Life, something big. What that was, he didn't know, but the promise of it was ripe, waiting to be revealed. Even though it was a mystery, it was *important*. It would change the future. And Olympia was crucial to it.

Sieg was still talking. "But back to Olympia. So, you read her all your stuff, but what do you *talk* about? You and Clara used to talk about everything."

Had they? From what Nate could remember, they'd both talked and neither had really listened. Last time he'd seen her, she'd insulted his poetry. She wasn't interested in his art other than his dreamscapes, and he couldn't understand half of what she said. Yes, the crush had been short-lived. It was obvious they weren't meant to be together.

"Well, nothing really. I talk, and she listens."

"She *listens*? That's all? I mean, that's got to be great at first, Nate, but how long can it last? I like the sound of my own voice as much as the next guy, but still, every so often you want a two-sided conversation, don't you?"

"Maybe you need someone to natter away in your ear mindlessly, Sieg, but I don't." Nate pushed himself away from his desk. "What good are words anyway? I might need them to express myself, but Olympia doesn't. Everything she needs to say she says with her eyes, with her body language. There's more sense in her way of speaking than anything said just to fill the silence."

"Nate, that's—"

"What? Crazy? How would you know, Sieg? You've never been in love before. If you had, you would know that words are only a small part of it. Clara used to speak to me incessantly, and I still had no idea what she was trying to say. With Olympia, a mere glance tells me everything I need to know."

His hands had clenched into fists in his lap. Had he once had similar doubts about Olympia? Part of his mind seemed to think so. But the other part chastised him for his disloyalty, his unworthiness. So what if she never spoke?

Lifting his eyes from Nate's hands, Sieg held up his own. "I'm sorry, Nate. I never meant to offend you. You're right—I've never been in love, not the way you are, anyway, so I don't know what it's like."

Somewhat mollified, Nate turned back to his work. "I hope that one day you are, my friend, though there are very few women like Olympia."

"That I can agree with." Sieg paused and glanced casually out the window. "So, what does Spalazani make of all this?"

"He's pleased. And why wouldn't he be?" Nate spun around in his chair again, his eyes narrowing.

"No reason. Nate, man, you need to relax. I was just making conversation."

Nate couldn't explain his sudden irritation, nor why Sieg's presence was no longer welcome. "If you want to know so much about him, why don't you go ask him yourself? Or better yet, go talk to one of his cronies and stop bothering me."

"Nate, you're the one who asked for my help, remember?" Sieg stood. "But if this is the way you're going to act, I've got better things to do."

"Fine, get out of here then. I'll get more done without you pestering me, anyway."

Without another word, Sieg turned on his heel and left, slamming the door so hard that it leaped on its hinges.

What the hell was up with Sieg? Why was he always trying to tear him and Olympia down? It wasn't Nate's fault Sieg couldn't understand a woman like Olympia. All the women he normally associated with talked so much because they were worried if they stopped, everyone would find out just how insipid they really were. But not his Olympia. She'd hold her tongue until she had something important to say. A mind as keen and a soul as heavenly as hers had no need to speak. Nate understood her well enough, and those who didn't, didn't deserve to.

Why couldn't anyone else see what a remarkable woman she was?

Perhaps it's for the best. Would I really want the competition? I've got a lot to offer her, but... A layer of permafrost settled like a band around Nate's stomach.

But what if she met someone else? Someone less fumbling, less flawed. Until now, Olympia had seen only one or two sides to Nate—the sides he wanted her to see. That had been part of the problem with his crush on Clara. They'd shared everything, known everything about each other, including their faults. Once, that in-depth knowledge had seemed important, even necessary to the success of their relationship, but Nate didn't want Olympia to see all of him.

What if she found one of his habits unpleasant? Loth and Clara had ribbed him, albeit good-naturedly, about his messiness, his quick temper, his mercurial moods, his thoughtlessness. What if Olympia saw these traits in him and found him wanting?

His horror mounted as he considered the possibilities. Another man, someone who didn't have these weaknesses, who was undamaged. What then? Would she cast him aside? He would never survive it. *I have to act quickly, or I might lose my love forever.* Good thing he had a plan.

***

The next night, as he left Professor Spalazani's house and the company of the woman he adored, he asked the older man to step outside with him.

"Of course, Nathanael." He closed the door behind them, and they stood in the twilight, their breath coiling faintly around their heads in the cool air. "What can I help you with? Are you getting behind in your work again?"

"No, sir, nothing like that." In truth, he was, but that wasn't what he wanted to speak to the professor about.

Nausea burned the back of his throat, oddly familiar.

Why was he so nervous? He'd been so sure when the idea had crossed his mind last night. All day, he'd hardly been able to wait for this moment to come.

So why am I hesitating?

A familiar voice clawed at his mind, calling from a dormant place in the heart he'd thought wholly devoted to Olympia.

Don't do this, Nate. This woman, she isn't what you think. None of this is what you think. It's a dream, nothing more. An insidious lie.

But how could it be? All evening, Olympia had sat next to him, her eyes burning with what could only be affection as she'd listened wordlessly to his most recent sonnet in her honor. There was no mistaking it.

It's nerves, nothing more.

Yet, he'd been here before, hadn't he? Felt similar fear of unrequited love? He didn't have to worry about that with Olympia; surely, he knew how she felt. The other time it had been a dream, a childish dream he'd let go of.

"Nate?" Professor Spalazani peered up at Nate in the soft light of the porch. "Are you quite all right?"

What was he doing here? "I— I don't—"

"Was it about Olympia?" The older man placed a kind hand on his arm. "My daughter?"

Olympia. Yes, that's it. Olympia, his beloved.

"Yes, sir. I—" The words caught in his throat.

Why was this so difficult? It was as though some outside force was working against him, trying to silence him so he and Olympia would never be together. Pain lanced the back of his eyes and he fought to keep from covering them with his hands.

He tried again, determined to get through it even if the effort killed him. "Sir, I would… That is, if you…" He took a deep, shuddering breath. "I would like to ask Olympia to marry me, sir, if you would be kind enough to give me your permission." The urge to sink to his knees almost overwhelmed him then, and only the relief of finally speaking kept him upright.

Spalazani gazed at him, impassive.

Nate's stomach sank. *He doesn't think I'm worthy. And maybe he's right. Maybe I—*

The professor's face broke into a large grin, and he slapped Nate on the back. "Nate, my boy! I was wondering when you were going to ask."

"Does that mean, sir," Nate fought to keep his voice level, "that you approve?"

"Absolutely. I couldn't ask for a better match for my dear Olympia." He shook Nate's hand. "As long as she agrees, that is."

"Do you…do you think she will, sir?"

"I have no doubt, my boy. I see the way she looks at you. She's a special girl, my Olympia, and not everyone is capable of seeing it. I'm glad, so glad that you can."

Were those tears in the other man's eyes? Tears of joy? They must be.

Why was I so nervous?

He shook the professor's hand vigorously, eager now to get home and revel in his victory. Spalazani seemed to understand his urgency and shook his hand firmly once more. "Get some sleep, Nathanael. I'll make sure Olympia is available all day tomorrow so that you can make your proposal." His brow furrowed. "You *were* planning to do it soon, weren't you?"

"I—" He hadn't been, really, not until he had more time to prepare a proposal worthy of such a woman, but with Spalazani's eager face before him, there wasn't a single good reason to delay. So what if the proposal wasn't a grand gesture of fireworks and champagne? It would come from his heart. And if he knew Olympia as well as he thought he did, a modest proposal was much more her style.

"Yes, sir. Tomorrow. I will be here at the break of dawn."

Spalazani's face flushed, and he squeezed Nate's hand yet again. "Excellent, excellent, my boy. I— I cannot tell you how grateful I am, Nathanael, that you should wish to bring my only daughter such happiness." And with that, he gave Nate's hand one more shake then left.

Nate soared back home. Everything was settling into place. Maybe the dark curse he'd been living under was finally lifting.

Back in his room, he took a box down from his closet shelf and sat on his bed to pour over the contents. On the top was a folded slip of paper, faintly scented like fresh citrus. *What's this?* He unfolded it to reveal a letter of childish scrawl as familiar to him as his own.

Dear Nate,

I'm so sorry to hear about your father. I can't imagine what you're feeling right now. I tried to visit you today, but you were still ill, so I made Bunty promise to give you this note—I told her I would tell your mother that she's been filching the sugar pigs out of the pantry if she didn't. Loth and I will be coming to the funeral, and we'll sit together. We'll get through this, Nate, even if it doesn't seem like it right now. I promise. Together, we can get through anything, even death.

Love, Clara.

It was a note he'd often read in his darkest moments of doubt about why he was here at the university, one of the few things that could break his fits of despair. *Together, we can get through anything.* And they always had. Until now.

Smiling at the grave child Clara had been, he tossed the letter aside without a second glance. Underneath it was a photograph of him, Clara, and Loth, the three of them dressed for some function or another, wide gaps where their baby teeth had fallen out and their faces ruddy with health. It followed the letter onto the floor and under the bed.

What he was searching for was far more important. And there it was, in the bottom corner of the lacquered box.

A ring. The one his father had given his mother on the day of their engagement. His mother had given it to him last year, just before he went away. At the time, he'd thought perhaps it was a hint, but now he recognized it for what it was: a mother's foresight. Perhaps she'd known he'd meet his true love here, away from home, and she'd wanted him to be prepared. He should call and thank her sometime.

He turned the slim platinum band over in his fingers. It had been intended for another, once. It seemed so long ago, his emotions so simple compared to what they were now. The blood-red stone in the center reflected his face back at him, and for once, he was the man he'd always wanted to be.

How beautiful it will look on her elegant finger.

He spent the next thirty minutes in front of his full-length mirror, practicing. One knee or two? Should he plead? Would the tears in his eyes be welcome? Or should he sweep in commandingly and present it with a flourish, no words needed?

Unable to decide, he placed the ring on his bedside table. Perhaps he would dream of the ideal proposal, one worthy of his future wife. He lay down and switched off the light, the vision of her etched on his eyelids in glorious relief.

Tomorrow, all his dreams would come true.

SEVENTEEN

The church bells pealed out over the water, reverberating through Clara's skull. The happy couple burst through the entranceway, hand-in-hand, showered by millions of tiny glittering stars thrown by the cheering crowd.

Olympia smiled modestly at the adulation, her veil thrown back over her head and her cheeks flushed a becoming pink. The flush in Nate was darker, almost feverish. His grip on Olympia's hand was that of a drowning man, yet she didn't cry out, bearing it with little more than a sigh.

They ran through the parting crowd down to the edge of the lake, which, in their honor, remained as still and clear as a pane of glass. The grasses and reeds at the shoreline stood straight to attention, and even the sky had blessed their union, cloudless, and blue, and eternally day. A small boat sat moored on the water's edge, elaborately painted with gilt and festooned with massive chrysanthemums.

As they stood on the shore, Olympia raised her arm and pointed out over the lake. "Do you see that, Nathanael? Everything before us?"

"Yes." Nate's eyes didn't follow his bride's finger but remained fixed on her face. Any will to look away from her had deserted him at last. He'd *surrendered, wholly and completely. Clara's heart threatened to break, even as his own swelled.*

"That is our future. Look." She pressed her hand to the side of his face to turn his head. His eyes strained to stay on her face, but at last, with a strangled cry of regret, he acquiesced and joined his bride in looking out over the water.

"What is?" Nothing was there but a vast, empty ocean stretching out to the horizon.

"Anything you believe." Her voice had an odd, discordant quality, an almost masculine edge, as though another voice had blended with hers. "With your resources, we can do anything."

His resources? What an odd thing to say. It certainly wasn't the speech of love Clara would've expected from a new bride. It must be Coppelius at work. Perhaps the bastard would give more of his intentions away. Come on, you old monster. Keep talking.

"What would you have us do, my love? Everything that's mine is yours." Even in his dreams, Nate's speech was as flowery and trite as his recent poetry.

Olympia smiled, a wolfish grin that stretched her face unnaturally, and the grass at her feet shuddered. "But you must agree, Nathanael, that you will never go back. You can never go back. If you do, it will kill me."

Nate snatched up his bride's hands in his own and clutched them to his chest. "Don't speak like that, please, my love. I can't bear the thought of you being anything but here with me, right now. Whatever you want, I'll do it."

"We will get into this boat and cross this lake, Nathanael. And once we do, you can never go back."

His only desire was to go forward, and quickly, away from this place. There was something here he had to get away from. Something merciless. "I won't, I promise you. I have nothing to go back for. Nothing. You are my life, my love, my only love."

"Take one last look then, because this is the last time you will ever see your old life, my dear. Take one look then make your decision." She pointed back the way they'd come.

The church was in ruins, the stone walls caving in on themselves, and the bell, which had rung so joyously only a short time before, had cracked in two, never to be rung again. The ground around the church lay wasted, all burned and salted earth, and a choking ash hung thick in the air.

Among the barren, blackened ruins stood Clara, reaching for Nate, her voice a beseeching wail. Dirt and ash smudged her sour, unkind face and tattered clothing, and her fingers were tipped with blood.

Nate clapped his hands over his ears and dropped to his knees. One hand stretched out toward Clara's dream-twin then dropped back down to the earth, where he clenched a fistful of dirt. The grains slipped between his fingers, carried away on the wind. And yet, this dirt was real, as were these ruins. And comforting, somehow—

"Why are you fighting, Nate? I thought you wanted this."

"I do. I just... I want...Clara." That was right. Clara. Not this woman next to him. How had he forgotten her?

Olympia frowned as though dealing with a naughty child. "Clara will be fine, Nathanael. She doesn't need you. She never has."

That's not true, *Clara tried to shout inside him, but an errant wind snatched the words from his mouth.* I do need you. I always have. We need each other.

"*You see all this destruction around you, Nate? Do you?*"

He nodded. So much devastation.

"*This is what Clara has wrought. And she will ruin you too. If you look back, your life will be over. Her conditional love will grind you down until you're nothing but dust, a dead man inside a young body.*" *Olympia grasped Nate by the hair and rocked his head back.* "*Is that what you want? To keep dying every day, over and over, until death itself feel like a gift?*"

Nate swallowed and choked against the angle of his neck. "*No. No, I don't want that, but—*"

"*Look at me, Nathanael. Look at what I'm offering you.*"

He turned his eyes toward her, a vision of life and beauty. She'd grown even more radiant while he'd been looking away, and now her beauty was almost painful. She guided his face gently toward the lake again, and he gazed out over the shining water to the city now glittering on the horizon.

"*That city will be ours. We will change the world beyond its wildest dreams. We will rule the Blackmoth Republic, Nathanael. With your assets and my mind, we will be unmatched.*"

Your assets and my mind. There it was again. Coppelius was getting desperate, to be so blunt. He must feel Nate fighting him, his victory no longer a sure thing.

"*You must choose now, Nathanael. Choose between the life you see behind you, or the one in front of you. Take a leap of faith, or else be stuck in limbo, stuck in a war between duty and the true feelings of your heart.*"

Nate clutched at Olympia's skirts and buried his face in them. "I— I choose you, Olympia."

She turned her head to where dream-Clara stood, her lips pulled back from her teeth in an ugly snarl of victory, and Clara's heart turned to glass.

She'd lost him. Her Nate, her love. She hadn't been enough for him. Hadn't fought hard enough, passionately enough. She'd given in to logic and reason, had underestimated the fragility of his heart. It was over.

Then Coppelius pushed his advantage too far.

"You must prove yourself to me."

Nate gazed up her, uncomprehending. "What do you mean? I've married you. I've forsaken everything for you."

"Kill her." She pointed a tremulous finger at dream-Clara. A sword appeared in her hand, a long platinum blade set in a hilt studded with blood-red stones.

A sword, Coppelius? Really? *The ridiculous pompousness of it all would've made Clara laugh, if they weren't currently fighting over Nate's soul.*

Nate recoiled from Olympia, his gut twisting in horror, as though he'd begun to see her for what she was. Yes, Nate. Fight. *"What? No. I can't. I won't. I've already hurt her enough."*

"You will, or I'll use this sword to take my own life." Olympia raised the heavy blade to her throat and drew a line across her skin. Clara held her breath, waiting for the blood to flow from the young woman's neck. None came.

Still, it had the desired effect. Confused, Nate gave a strangled cry and leaped to his feet, wresting the sword away from Olympia before she could raise it again. Then he turned toward dream-Clara, who waited in the ruins, gazing at him with soulless eyes.

No. Keep fighting her, Nate. For us.

Nate walked back toward the ruin of his life, to the architect of his destruction standing in the center. He stood in front of her as she stared back impassively, no hint of love anywhere in her face. She was cold and distant. Uncaring.

Is this how he sees me? Or is this purely Coppelius's doing?

No wonder Olympia, despite her strangeness, seemed like a haven.

A woman who doesn't even speak has shown him more love than I. Or so he believes.

And he did, despite his uncertainty.

She had to stop this now, had to show him that she did love him. That she always had. Perhaps it would get through to him, to his subconscious. She could stop this madness if, for once, she just abandoned logic.

His chest was heaving as he raised the sword high over his head. Dream-Clara didn't react, but stared stonily ahead, as though her own impending death at the hands of the love of her life was of little consequence to her, just another of Nate's emotional outbursts to be endured.

As he brought the sword down on dream-Clara's neck, he had a moment of clarity. "Help me, Clara. Please. If you can hear me, please, stop this."

The sword cleaved dream-Clara's head from her shoulders, and as it tumbled into the ashen curve of the broken bell, he drove the sword point first into the ground and wept.

He strode back down the hill toward Olympia, waiting triumphantly at the bottom. She held out her hands as he reached her and kissed each of his palms in turn. "You see? That wasn't so hard, was it? Now you are free, Nathanael, to become."

"What will I become?" A numbness had filled his chest, and Clara recoiled at the sheer nothingness of it. *She could never have imagined anyone being so cruel, to have the will to so pitilessly destroy another person. Her person.*

Good, Clara. Get mad.

Nate, her Nate, was still in there. He wanted to get back to her.

You will, Nate. I'll get you back.

Nate and Olympia climbed into the boat. As they pushed away from the shore, Nate's gaze once again returned to Olympia, alternating between wariness and the rabid devotion that made Clara want to scream until she turned herself inside out. Olympia, for her part, kept her gaze on the headless body of dream-Clara, slumped over a block of stone. A malicious smile curved her lips. She had won.

Oh no you don't, bitch. You haven't won anything yet. *Coppelius, she corrected herself. For all Clara knew, Olympia was just as much a victim in this as she was.*

Enjoy it while you can, Coppelius, because I'm coming for you.

EIGHTEEN

Clara scrolled through page after page, gleaning every bit of information about the enemy she could. Blood still roared in her ears every time she thought about Nate's dream, about what Coppelius had made Nate do. But by asking Nate to kill Clara, he'd pushed him too hard and momentarily broken the spell. He'd underestimated Nate's love for Clara.

And so had she.

Well, she wasn't going to make that mistake again. Nate was still in there, and he'd asked for her help. She had no doubt that the only thing in immediate danger was his heart and soul, but to her, that was everything.

Coppelius was a crafty bastard. Even though she'd searched for hours, she'd found very little information on him. There were numerous reports of his early career, images of him and Nate and Clara's fathers smiling into the cameras, a gangly Ari hovering in the background almost out of frame. He was later mentioned as being wanted by police as a witness in the death of Nate's father since he was the last one to see him alive, and then...nothing. No family announcements, job promotions, awards, none of the usual trail people left behind.

Except for his obituary.

According to the most recent source she could find, Coppelius had died five years ago, in a mysterious accident beyond the Perimeter. His belongings had been recovered, but his body had never been found, assumed to have been lost to the monsters that roamed there. It wasn't an unusual fate in Foxwept Province for those foolish enough to cross the border. A picture accompanied his obituary, and although grainy, and slightly out of focus, his features were as Nate had described them in his letter, and his green eyes glared superciliously back at the camera, defiant from beyond the grave.

He's not dead. I know he's not dead. He's Vandran.

But on Vandran, she could find nothing. Not even a picture.

Until Sieg, glorious, wonderful Sieg, came through for her.

Here. I managed to get this image from the security cameras around campus. This is the guy that came to our house, just before Nate really started going off the deep end. Oh, and Spalazani's real name is Hoffman. No idea why or when he changed it, but there you go. Hope that helps. Let me know if you need anything else. Sieg.

Her fingers trembled over the keys as she messaged back. *Oh my god, Sieg, thank you so much! How did you find out about Spalazani?*

His reply came back only seconds later. *A gentleman never reveals his sources, but let's just say that the Red Dove isn't just sordid entertainment. You really should get out and let your hair down more, Clara. Sometimes even the real world can teach you things.*

The Red Dove? Wasn't that a bordello? *Does it matter, Clara? If this information pays off, you're taking Sieg there on an all-expenses-paid night out. And you will smile the entire time because it will have given Nate back to you.*

She took a deep breath. *Coppelius first.* The image Sieg had sent her was much clearer than the obituary footage. The man in it was not Coppelius. His nose was different, and his face was much thinner, but his eyes...his eyes were the same. The same off-green, tilted like a cat's. It was him—Vandran *was* Coppelius.

She called Ari on the comm.

"Hello?"

"Hi, Ari. It's Clara. Are you busy?"

"I'm always busy, Miss Clara, but what do you need? Have you found something?"

"I have. Can you come to my office, please?"

"Of course. I'll be right there. I have some information of my own." She hung up abruptly. Clara approved.

So Vandran was definitely Coppelius, and he was responsible for what was happening to Nate. But how were Spalazani and Olympia involved?

Clara hesitated as she typed in *Hoffman,* Spalazani's true name. What if it also came up blank? What would she do then?

But she needn't have worried. His name came up, as did Olympia's.

Ari's sharp knock brought her back to her senses. How long had she been sitting there, staring at the screen in horror? She swallowed around the dryness in her throat. "Come in."

Ari did, shutting the door firmly behind her. One look at Clara's face and she rushed to her side, dropping the armful of papers she'd been carrying.

"Miss Clara! What's happened? Is it Nathanael? Has something more—"

Wordlessly, Clara pointed at her screen. Ari bent over and scrutinized the article, her eyes flicking rapidly back and forth as she skimmed it.

"Hoffman? Who is—"

"Spalazani. Keep reading."

Soon Ari's expression changed. From sympathy, to shock, to confusion as she connected the same dots Clara had.

According to the article, Daniel Hoffman had one child, a daughter named Olympia. A picture of the two of them was included halfway down. He was a handsome, supercilious-looking man with dark hair shot through with silver at his temples. His arm was wrapped around the shoulders of a young woman, about eighteen years old, with rich auburn hair and a somber expression. It was definitely the woman from Nate's dreams, the one Sieg had confirmed was *the* Olympia who'd stolen Nate's heart. Her image glared up at Ari and Clara with all the suppressed wrath of a young woman unwillingly burdened with the crown of a kingdom.

The expression was familiar. *She looks like me.* Clara had worn that exact expression at her debutante ball. It was the day she'd officially inherited Dreaming Life. She'd known the day was coming, but she hadn't been able to mask her feelings. All she'd ever wanted was to be a scientist— and not a dream scientist—losing herself in theories and experiments, not being responsible for an empire.

Olympia, it seemed, was meant to meet a similar fate. She was a daughter of the Golden Isle, a private island for the grossly wealthy, secluded and protected from the riffraff of Foxwept Province.

Owning a home there was by invitation alone, an invitation Clara's parents had turned down with a laugh, preferring to live close to their beloved Portfade where they could witness their work first-hand. Even so, Clara understood all too well the torture of being trotted out in high society like a performing monkey when all she really wanted to do was hole up with her books.

As far as she could tell, there was only one major difference between her and Olympia.

Olympia was *dead*. Sorrow rose cold and sharp in Clara's throat.

The article was a synopsis of Hoffman's glittering career, the loss of his only daughter reduced to a single paragraph. Clara pulled up another article, and the two women read it together.

Olympia had had her own dreams as well—dreams that weren't in line with what her father wanted for her. She'd wished to be a soldier on the Perimeter, fighting the monsters created by the Goldhare Horizon disaster.

A common soldier risking her life on the front line? Not if her father had anything to do with it. He'd kept her locked up like the archetypal princess in a tower, guarding her jealously from the outside world and all its temptations. Her mother had died when she was just a child, and Olympia became his sole focus.

Ari shook her head. "Imagine having to live like that."

She'd died in an accident shortly after the picture had been taken, according to the article. One night, she'd gotten it into her head that her only choice was to steal a boat, bypass the controls, and flee. She would assume a false name and then, a free woman, join the Foxwept military and fulfill her dreams. She would fight for her country and fellow citizens.

"I get it, you know." And Clara really did. She too could've lived a life of endless indulgence and superficial philanthropy, but she'd wanted to do something that mattered. Not just to the world at large, but to *herself*.

"I do too. I mean, I came from much humbler beginnings, but even then, I made a choice not to give in to the hand I'd been dealt." Ari shook her head again. "What a shame she never got the chance to make her difference."

Clara continued reading. "So she was heading across the Ghostlight to Portfade when she crashed into another boat. The other people survived, but she didn't. She was on life support for a few weeks before succumbing to her injuries." *The poor woman.* "It's so sad."

Ari cleared her throat. "Miss Clara, I agree, it is. But at the risk of sounding insensitive...if Olympia is dead, who is *Olympia*?"

Ari was right. Clara sighed, frustrated. For the life of her, she still couldn't see the connection. What the hell linked Hoffman and Coppelius? Who was the woman posing as Spalazani's daughter? And why had Spalazani changed his name?

Clara dropped her face into her hands, exhausted. "I just can't figure it out, Ari. What are we missing?"

The older woman was no less baffled. "I have no idea. I—"

An alert pinged on Clara's screen. *Sieg.*

We need to talk.

A moment later, Clara accepted his call. The normally effervescent young man looked uncharacteristically grim.

"Sieg? Is everything all right? You'll never guess what I found out. Spalazani is—"

"About to become Nate's father-in-law."

"What?" The words ricocheted around her brain, too fast for her to catch.

"Nate, that idiot, is about to propose to Olympia. I tried to talk him out of it, but he's beyond listening. He's got a ring and everything. A platinum band with—"

"A single red stone." *The ring Nate insisted would be mine one day.* He'd still been a child when he'd made that promise, but Clara had believed it with all her heart. She'd even tried it on one day, the slim band fitting her finger perfectly. "Sieg, you have to stop him."

"I *tried*, Clara. I really did. But he's not listening to reason."

"You have to try again." Clara quickly filled Sieg in on Hoffman's past.

"Wait, so Olympia is dead? I mean, she's pretty stiff, but—"

"Sieg! This isn't a joke. I think Nate is in danger. You need to stop him. Whatever it takes. Tie him to a chair if you have to."

Sieg winced as though he'd tasted something bitter. "Okay, I'll try. But I can't guarantee anything. I'm a lover, not a fighter."

"Just do what you can. Now. And keep in touch."

"Will do." His face disappeared from the screen. If only she had more confidence in him.

Should I take a chopper to Draglight? Would I even get there in time? But that wasn't her biggest worry. What if she got there only to find that Nate wasn't in the grip of the Sandman, but was truly in love with Olympia, truly wanted her to be his wife?

That's what you're really afraid of.

Keeping him at arm's length all these years had been a defense as much as anything. Clara, who'd met every problem in her life head-on, couldn't bear confronting Nate and finding out the truth she'd feared all along: that he didn't love her the way she did him.

Snap out of it, Clara. Stop being so selfish. If you truly loved him as much as you claim, you'd get on that chopper right now and get your ass to that island. Because whether he loves you or not, he's in trouble, and he needs you.

Whatever Coppelius had planned was connected to Olympia. He wanted Nate to marry Olympia, even if Clara couldn't yet figure out why. That meant his plan was coming to a head. She didn't know what she would do, but she couldn't let him win.

"Ari? Would you like to go for a ride?"

NINETEEN

Nate checked his reflection in the mirror one more time. His face was flushed, and his eyes shone.

That's the face of a man in love. A man about to become happier than he's been in his entire life.

Why then, did unease gnaw at the corners of his mind? At the bottom of his heart? Was it because he'd known Olympia such a short time? Was it because he hadn't told his own mother about the love of his life? Or his friends Lothair and Clara? Well, they would be thrilled for him when they found out. This was just the engagement, after all. They could come to the wedding. Hell, they could be the guests of honor.

What if she says no?

But why would she? She'd given him every indication that she was as in love with him as he was with her, and he had her father's blessing.

No, you're just getting cold feet, Nate. But you have no reason to. This is what you've wanted all your life.

He'd never wanted anything more. His devotion surprised him. The only other thing in his life he'd never questioned was his love for Clara. Well, crush. What he felt now for Olympia proved that.

Stop stalling.

Was he just drawing out the anticipation, reveling in it? It was unlike him. Clara had always teased him about his impatience.

Clara. There she was again. Why couldn't he stop thinking about her? On this day, of all days?

It's your nerves, nothing more. You're petrified about becoming an honest man, and falling back on what's familiar and easy. So stop it, and go. Go and get the woman of your dreams.

He grinned at himself one last time then checked his pocket for the ring.

He'd just opened the front door when a hand shot over his shoulder and pushed it shut. He spun around. Sieg.

"What do you want?" The irritation in his voice caught even him by surprise.

"You can't do this, Nate. Olympia isn't who you think she is."

"This again? It's not funny, Sieg."

"I'm not laughing. I'm serious, Nate. I just spoke to Clara, and—"

"You tattled to my ex-crush about me? Are you serious?"

"Nate, she's worried about you! And I don't blame her, the way you've been acting, tossing your entire life aside for a woman who can't even string a sentence together. I—"

Nate's fist connected with Sieg's jaw, sending him reeling into the wall. "Don't speak about Olympia like that ever again. She's going to be my wife, and to hell with the rest of you." He stalked out the door, leaving Sieg in a heap, rubbing his tender jaw.

When he arrived at Spalazani's, the front door was ajar. Had the professor left it open for Nate so he could sneak in and surprise Olympia? How thoughtful of him. But as Nate pushed it open, as quietly as he could, raised voices from the main parlor greeted him. Two voices, both male, one enraged and one pleading. What the hell was going on? Where was Olympia? His heart in his throat, Nate followed the voices.

The parlor was in ruins, the furniture overturned, the elegant glass coffee table in pieces strewn across the floor. Two men grappled over a prone form on the floor, a woman with striking auburn hair. *Olympia!*

Unseen, Nate started to rush to her side then froze as he recognized the combatants. One was, of course, Olympia's father. The other...the other was the manifestation of Nate's childhood fears.

Coppelius. *The Sandman.*

He was still dressed as Vandran, but he could disguise his true nature no longer. His face was distorted with rage, the way it had been the night he'd discovered Nate hiding in his father's laboratory. Nate had been right all along. But what was he doing here?

Coppelius was screaming into Spalazani's face. A large vein pulsed in his neck, and his features were purple with rage. "You promised! You promised they'd be married by now!"

Spalazani was clearly on the losing end of the fight, the corner of his mouth leaking blood as he tried to wrest Coppelius's meaty hands from his collar. "They will be! He's going to propose today, I'm sure of it. I—"

"No! It's too late. It's over. I'm taking these with me." He brandished something in his hands, something that made Spalazani blanch and shriek with anguish.

"No! You can't! You promised! You—"

"Your time's run out! Someone's onto us, you fool. You had your chance." He twisted Spalazani's collar between his fingers, and the professor began to choke. "I can't get caught. Do you have any idea what would happen to me? I was close, so close, and then you ruined it!" He gave Spalazani a shake, and the professor's head jerked violently on his neck. "You should've pushed him harder. You and that corpse child of yours." With one last push, he tossed Spalazani to the ground.

"Please," Spalazani pleaded from the floor. "Please, just leave them with me. I'll get you your money, I promise. Just leave me the eyes. She needs them."

The eyes. The room started to spin.

"No. I made them—they're mine. We had a deal. No money, no eyes. I'll finish this myself." And with that, Coppelius spun on his heel and stalked away, his shoes grinding shards of glass into the glossy marble floor.

Spalazani crawled after him, screaming wordlessly, his hands bleeding from a dozen cuts. Halfway across the room, he gave up and collapsed facedown, sobbing.

But Nate had eyes only for Olympia. He staggered over to where she lay, and ignoring Spalazani, put his hand on her shoulder. "Olympia? My love? Are you all right?"

As usual, she said nothing, but this silence was different, not the silence of a profound spirit, but of shock and pain. Her hands were raised to her face, covering her eyes.

The eyes. The eyes.

"Olympia?" When she didn't move, Nate took a deep breath, placed his hands over hers, and tried one more time. "My love?"

Slowly, he pulled her hands away.

A scream of anguish burst from his lips. Smooth, empty sockets stared back at him, the soft, synthetic skin marred in the center by protruding connections and torn filaments.

I don't...

As he struggled to make sense of what he was seeing, a shower of sparks exploded from her left eye socket, searing his lips and breaking the months-long spell.

He didn't love her. He never had. Who, *what* was this creature before him? Was it even alive? How had—

Coppelius.

A sob rose from behind him.

Spalazani, his shirt torn at the shoulder, had lurched to his feet and over to his daughter, reaching out for her. "Olympia."

Coppelius. *And this man.* They'd done something to Nate—tricked him, forced him into— He'd almost married whatever this mannequin was. They'd manipulated him, nearly made him throw away everything he loved. His life, his family, his—

Clara.

What had this done to Clara? She must know, must believe that he was in love with another woman, was about to propose to her with the ring. *Her* ring.

Nate launched to his feet and barreled into his professor, striking him hard in the chest with his shoulder. Winded, Spalazani reeled backward, crashing into one of the few tables left standing. Caught between it and Nate's fury, he raised his hands to try to shield himself as Nate rained down blows wherever he could reach, the sickening thud of his fists against the other man's soft flesh overwhelmed by the roaring in his ears.

"Nate, stop!"

The voice was female, and he glanced wildly around. He knew that voice.

"Nate," the voice screamed again. "*Nate!*"

Olympia still lay where he'd left her. So who could it be?

Clara?

Spalazani slid to the floor, his face a bloody pulp.

The room spun faster and faster, a blur Nate could no longer focus on. In truth, he didn't even want to try. Happily, he gave himself up to it, embracing the darkness that rushed up to greet him like an old friend.

TWENTY

BEATEN PROFESSOR STILL RECOVERING IN
HOSPITAL
*In a sequence of events right out of a story, noted
professor Daniel Spalazani continues to recover in
Portfade Hospital today after being savagely beaten
in his own home by an unnamed student...*

Clara threw the newspaper across the room in
disgust. "Can you believe it? Making him out to be
some kind of victim?"

"Well, technically, he was, ma'am." The officer's
lips were pursed primly, and Clara fought the urge
to un-purse them with the back of her hand. How
dare the policewoman try to absolve him? He was
just as much to blame as Coppelius. And even worse,
Olympia was his daughter, for god's sake. The man
was a monster.

"No, he wasn't. Nate was only—"

"We've been over this, m—"

"Stop calling me ma'am. My name is Clara."

"Sorry, Clara. But we've been over this. The law
deals in technicalities, and Nate did beat this man
within an inch of his life, whatever his motivations
were." Her ruddy face softened. "I'm not saying that
I disagree with what Nathanael did, but I do have to
follow the law."

The officer's reasonableness infuriated Clara. "But what's going to happen to Nate?" The police had wanted to charge him with attempted murder, but the story Clara had told them was so fantastical that they allowed Nate to be taken to the hospital for a scan. Arienne had pointed out the chips in Nate's head and explained in great detail about the unusual electrical signals they emitted, evidence of what Coppelius had done. Between that and Olympia herself, it was all the proof they needed that Nate had not been entirely responsible for his actions.

"Nathanael will have to be charged. But, given the circumstances, all involved have agreed that if he pleads guilty, he can serve his sentence under house arrest, here at Dreaming Life. Even though he wasn't directly under the control of this Coppelius at the time of the beating—isn't that right?" She squinted at her screen

"We think so. We believe that when Coppelius...when he removed Olympia's eyes, it broke the connection between Nate and Olympia. We *think* that's how Coppelius was transmitting the signal. Nate said things changed after that, that he felt different, and there's been no interference in his dreams since. He seems pretty much back to normal, although..."

Although he's devastated, guilty, embarrassed, angry....and scared.

The officer sighed. "We still have to find Coppelius. That's part of why we have to go through with charging Nathanael. At the moment, there's no proof he existed. Professor Spalazani swears he doesn't know where he is, and the hospital won't let us anywhere near Olympia, though they've promised to let us know if she reveals anything." She raised her eyebrow in stern amusement and shook her head as Loth waved his bottle of lucéat at her. "To be honest, I'm still having trouble understanding what happened. I've never seen anything like this."

"You're not the only one." Loth poured himself his usual draught and settled back against the cushions.

Clara frowned at him before turning back to the officer. "Did they tell you about Olympia? About what happened to her?"

At the hospital, Olympia had been admitted straight to the Dreaming Life wing. The police had warned Clara to stay away unless she was specifically requested, but they'd also agreed it was the most humane treatment option for her at the moment. Since her consciousness was in the body of an android, the police had no other ideas what to do with her.

"Her father spilled everything—except where Coppelius might be. After Olympia was in the accident, her father kept her on life support for weeks while he searched for a way to keep her alive. In a last frantic attempt, he found someone who was able to transfer Olympia's consciousness from her ruined body."

"But it didn't work."

"No. It was a temporary measure only, like a life support for her...soul, I guess you could say. It was the only way."

"They could have brought her to Dreaming Life. I'm sure we could have found a better solution."

"Apparently, Spalazani wanted to keep it secret. That's why he declared her dead, and why he later changed his name. Perhaps he believed it would simply be too high profile."

"It must've been expensive."

The officer nodded. "It was. And useless. Before long, her consciousness began to deteriorate, so they had to move it."

"And that's when they put her into the body of a non-sentient android?" Empathy squeezed Clara's chest. What had it been like for poor Olympia?

"Yes, an android body was his only choice."

"The scientist involved was trying to find the secret to immortality. He figured if they could successfully transplant her consciousness into an android's body, people could live forever." The officer looked faintly disgusted. "He was probably accepting his award in his head the entire time. These scientist types..." The officer grimaced and colored when she realized who she was talking to. "I don't mean—"

Clara dismissed it with a wave of her hand. "It's fine. Believe me, I don't disagree with you." *Even Nate's own father betrayed him for science.*

"How could a father do that to his own daughter?" Loth interjected, shuddering. "I mean—"

Clara looked away. "When you love someone, Loth, you'd do anything for them."

"But that? And come on, Clara, don't play devil's advocate here. You'd never do something like that, no matter how much you loved someone."

Wouldn't she? Clara wasn't so sure. At one time, she would've agreed with Loth wholeheartedly, but now, after coming so close to losing Nate... "You don't know until you're in that situation."

"Well, promise me that you'll never do that to me, Clara. I'm serious. If something like that happens to me, either let me go, or at the very most, plug me into a Dreaming Life unit. I'll leave it in my will which ones."

"I'm sure I can figure it out, Loth," Clara said dryly. "They'll be filed under 'D' for debauchery."

The officer cleared her throat. "I never would've thought someone could be so cruel, especially to their own child, no matter how desperate they were."

According to Arienne, Olympia had been trapped in a body that could move only as programmed, blind and deaf, her voice, which had so captivated Nate at the ball, merely a recording. Clara couldn't imagine anything more devastating for a vigorous young woman who'd planned a career as a soldier. "So her father needed another solution." Clara rose to her feet, restless. "And that was when he found Coppelius. Apparently, he'd spent his years in hiding doing some experimentation of his own."

"He implanted a pair of synthetic eyes into Olympia, which connected to her consciousness and allowed her to see, and he also improved her mobility." The officer spoke slowly, her eyes fixed on the ceiling, as though she was trying to remember what Ari had told her. "Coppelius figured that if it was successful, he was onto something. And of course, it was. So he made a deal with Hoffman that Olympia could keep her eyes in exchange for continued funding for whatever monstrous idea he had next."

"And that's where Nate came in." Clara walked to the bay window at the front of the room. A light drizzle was falling from the overcast sky, misting the glass with tiny droplets.

"Yes. Hoffman had burned through much of his fortune by this point—he'd spent so long trying to get his daughter back that he'd neglected his business and was close to bankrupt. So after he changed their names to protect their identities, he took the job at the university."

"Did Spalazani tell you how Coppelius found Nate?" Clara breathed onto the glass, obscuring her reflection.

"No, but I imagine it wasn't that difficult. Nathanael is rather notorious on the social scene," the officer pointed out. "It was probably on all the gossip sites. So Coppelius tracked him to Draglight and hatched his plan. Apparently, he had some kind of history with Nate's father?"

"He felt Nate's father had robbed him of some patents—and he refused to continue to let Coppelius experiment on his son."

"You mean Nate's father was involved?" The officer's eyebrows rose in astonishment.

"Yes, although I don't think he knew what Coppelius eventually intended." Clara winced. Nate's mother would be clutching her pearls right about now at this airing of the family's dirty laundry.

"So it was also a matter of revenge." Her tone suggested it was a familiar motive.

"I imagine it seemed like the perfect solution. Get his money and revenge at the same time." Loth swirled the little liquid left in his glass. "So he and Hoffman hatched the plan to get Nate to marry Olympia?"

The officer nodded. "He told us that if the marriage went through, not only would he be able to get Coppelius his money and his daughter would keep her eyes, but Coppelius would continue his research and give Hoffman a cut so that he could rebuild his fortune." She inclined her head and narrowed her eyes at Loth. "Plus, with a family as influential as Nathanael's behind Olympia, Hoffman thought she would be accepted into society the way she was, a human consciousness in an android body. He could come clean and tell the world what they'd done." She shook her head. "He probably saw himself as a hero. He could regain his position in society, and his daughter would no longer be a source of shame." She glanced between Clara and Loth, her mouth pinched as though they were responsible for the conceit of wealth.

Loth wasn't satisfied. "What I don't understand is that they thought Nate was just going to hand over his fortune to Coppelius. I mean, Nate's impulsive, but I just can't see him being willing to fund that sort of thing, especially not as part of Dreaming Life."

Clara's face darkened. "I don't think they ever intended to get Nate to hand it over, Loth. Given the way Coppelius can manipulate Nate, my guess is that he planned to drive him mad to the point he was committed to a mental hospital and Olympia and her father gained access to his fortune—or something even worse."

"You mean, kill him?"

"Who knows? I wouldn't put it past him, that's for sure. Nate thinks Coppelius killed his father, and after what's happened, I'm inclined to agree." She shuddered. "He's a monster."

"And poor Nate just walked right into the trap."

"Don't 'poor Nate' him. You have no idea how hard he fought Coppelius. That fight nearly destroyed his mind, Loth."

Loth had the grace to look chastened. "I know, I just still can't get my head around it."

"Nate fought so hard that Coppelius had to go back and do it again with a stronger signal. He fought so, so hard." The back of Clara's throat burned, but her eyes remained dry. Rage blazed so hot in her she was unlikely to ever cry again.

And it wasn't only Coppelius and Hoffman she was angry at. After they'd shown the officer to the door, promising to let her know if they discovered anything else, Clara rounded on her brother.

"Have you visited Nate yet? It's been more than three days."

Loth looked away, suddenly fascinated by something in the bottom of his glass. "Ahh, you know what's it like, Clara. I've been so busy."

"Bullshit. You're a coward."

"Excuse me? I'm not." But he wouldn't meet her eyes.

"Yes, you are. Nate is your best friend, practically your brother. He's been through hell and you can't even be bothered to go and see him. He needs you, Loth. He needs all of us right now."

Clara would never forget the sight that had greeted her on Draglight. After landing, she and Ari had taken a car to the university campus where Nate and Hoffman lived. As she'd pulled up outside, Sieg was standing in the middle of the road, wiping blood from a split in his lip.

She'd leaped out of the car and grabbed his arm. "Where's Nate?"

He'd pointed across the street to a stately home. The door was wide open and sounds of a struggle were clear.

"Call the police, Sieg," she'd called over her shoulder before rushing headlong in, Nate her only concern.

She found them in a room that looked like it had been ground zero for a small bomb. Overturned furniture was everywhere, and glass and ceramics littered the floor. The body of a young woman lay crumpled, while next to her, Nate towered over another man, raining heavy blows down on his bloody face. Clara barely recognized Nate, his expression so distorted with rage.

"Nate!" He'd glanced around at first, but then continued to pummel the object of his fury, whose head lolled from side to side with each blow. "*Nate!*"

It was Ari who'd finally stopped him. She walked calmly up behind him and reached for the top of his shoulder. Clara had held her breath, afraid Nate would turn and attack her as well. But Ari merely touched him, and he collapsed to the floor, unconscious.

"Ari!"

"Pressure point. I'll show you sometime." The older woman had grimaced. "I think we're going to be needing an ambulance."

Clara knelt next to the bloodied man on the floor and pressed her fingers to his neck. Despite what Nate had done to his face, his pulse felt strong. This must be Hoffman. "Mr. Hoffman," Clara leaned close to his ear, "help is on the way. We—"

"Coppelius." His voice was thick.

"What about him?"

"Was...here. He took...her eyes. Beautiful eyes."

Coppelius was here? Clara leaped to her feet. "Ari, keep an eye on Hoffman." She curled her fingers around a large shard of glass and hid it behind her back as she stalked from room to room, searching behind doors and in hidden alcoves. If Coppelius was still here, she would find him.

But Coppelius was gone.

Even the police were baffled at how little a trail he'd left. He'd vanished, and so had Clara's hopes of seeing him punished for what he'd done.

But at least Nate was free of his control. It would take time for him to recover, but Clara was determined to help him every step of the way, no matter how long it took.

"Well, if you're not a coward, Loth, then what is it?"

"I just... After the way he treated you..."

Clara made a face at him. "It wasn't him, Loth, you know that. Besides, I know you well enough to know that's not the whole truth. Or even close to it." She snatched the bottle away as he went for a refill. "Besides...he won't see me yet."

"What? What do you mean he won't see you?"

"He's refusing to see me. I don't know if it's because he feels guilty, or—" *Or if he's ashamed that I saw his most vulnerable moments. Or if he associates me with everything that happened and hates the sight of me. Or if he really does love Olympia, after all, and doesn't know how to tell me. Or...*

Stop, Clara. Stop. You need to keep believing in him. He'll see you when he's ready.

But waiting for him to be ready was so hard. Her hands itched to smash down his door and throw herself into his arms and weep and tell him everything she'd ever wanted to tell him. But that had never been Clara. No, Clara waited patiently. At the moment, Clara *hated* Clara.

She sighed. "Please, Loth. Please go see him. For me, if nothing else."

Loth pressed his hands over his face. "It's just...I'm afraid to see him like that, Clara. So...broken. I let him down. You knew something was wrong with him...and I just thought he was wrong. What does it say about me, about our friendship, that I didn't get it?" He exhaled into his palms. "And what if Nate's not the same person he was? What if the Nate we know is gone?" He dropped his hands into his lap and stared at them. "I don't think I could bear it."

"So you're not a coward then, just selfish?"

"Clara—"

It was overly harsh, but she wasn't in the mood to cajole Loth, not this time. "No, Loth. It's selfish. He might not be the same person he was, but he's still Nate. You can't throw away a lifelong relationship because *you* feel guilty. He'll never get back to being the old Nate if we abandon him. We're his best chance for recovery."

"I know. I know you're right. It's just hard."

"Yeah? Think about how hard it's been for him. Now *go*." She snatched the glass from his hand.

"All right, all right," Loth grumbled, rolling off the couch. "Do you have a message you want me to give him?"

"Just that I'm thinking of him, and I miss him. And that when he's ready...well, you know."

Loth saluted. "Yes, ma'am. I'll report back later." He clicked his heels together with a mock salute and left Clara to her thoughts.

I can't just sit around here doing nothing. She had to do something, anything.

Her comm buzzed. "Clara?"

"Yes?"

"The Portfade Hospital is on the line."

The hospital? Was there an issue with one of their products? Loth usually fielded these calls, but right now, Nate came first. "Loth's busy right now. Is there anything I can help them with?"

"They don't want Lothair, they want you. It's about a patient."

"And?"

"Her name is Olympia. She wants to speak with you."

TWENTY-ONE

Clara wandered down a path through the forest. She trailed her hands over the leaves of some low-slung branches, marveling at how real they felt. Pride coursed through her. This was some of Dreaming Life's best work.

At the end of the path stood a quaint log cabin, smoke coiling from the chimney. Outside on the grass, an auburn-haired young woman sat cross-legged on a picnic blanket, a tiny fawn curled up beside her.

Olympia.

"Hi." Clara stood awkwardly. How did one greet the woman who'd almost stolen the love of her life through no fault of her own?

"Hi." Olympia herself seemed unsure how to act.

Clara took a deep breath. "Can I sit down?"

"Please." Olympia gestured to the blanket, and Clara sat, mimicking the other woman's cross-legged pose.

She held out her hand. "I'm Clara."

"I know who you are." Her face was pinched, her expression strained.

Is she angry with me? Or Nate? Does she hate it here? "Olympia, I—"

"Thank you."

Thank you? It *sounded* genuine. Guilt flared for the horrible thoughts she'd had about Olympia. She'd been a pawn, just like Nate. "You're welcome, of course, but you don't need to thank me, Olympia, I—"

"Do you know how long it's been since I've been able to move properly? I mean, I know this isn't *real*, but it feels real, and that's more than I've had for years." She gave Clara a shy smile. "When I first got here, I just *ran*. Everywhere."

"Did you swim in the lake?"

Olympia laughed. "I did. It was wonderful." She stroked the fawn under its chin then gestured around the meadow. "What is this place? I mean, I know about Dreaming Life, but what is *this* place?"

"This program was commissioned about sixty-five years ago by the parents of a young girl named Rose, for her to live in while she was in a coma. My father became one of their scientists, and eventually, he bought the company and renamed it Dreaming Life. He kept adding to this program, improving it, so gradually that Rose didn't notice. Eventually, this was the finished product. When she woke from her coma last year, she donated the program to be used by whoever needed it. I thought you might find it a good fit until we could design one specifically for you."

"Does that mean I'm stuck here?" She drew her knees to her chest and wrapped her arms around them.

"No, of course not. But..." How could she say this delicately? "From what the doctors have told me, your options right now are pretty limited. Either you can go back to the body your father put you in or remain in one of these programs. I— I've taken

189

the liberty of setting up a trust for you, so that you can stay with us for as long as you want."

"You mean, stay here, forever?" Her expression was unreadable.

"No, just until… Well, to be honest, I don't know. Olympia, what your father did—"

Olympia scowled. "Was heinous. He's a monster. He did it for himself, not for me." Her fingers dug into her thighs.

He was trying to save you. But she could never say that out loud. "Regardless, there's nothing that can be done for you right now. There's never been a case like yours before. At least, not one anyone's heard about. If that technology ever becomes legal…"

"I won't go back to that body. I won't." Her shoulders trembled.

Clara put her hand on Olympia's. "You don't have to."

The other woman bowed her head, and tears dotted the back of her hands. "Thank you, again."

They sat in silence for a minute before Olympia dried her face on her sleeve. "Is Nathanael okay?" She pulled up a few blades of grass. "It was horrible what they did to him, controlling his mind like that. I heard everything that went on between my father and Coppelius. I would've stopped it if I could've, but…you know. They didn't care if I consented to their plan or not." She glanced down at the blades in her hand. "I did try to warn him, but…" She shook her head and pressed her hand to her throat.

"It's okay, Olympia, I understand. And so will Nate, believe me. He won't blame you." Clara hated herself for what she was about to ask next, but she had to know. "Olympia…did…do you have feelings for Nate? I mean, I know that, given the situation, love was probably the last thing on your mind, but…

God, I'm sorry, I don't know why I'm asking you this." She covered her face with her hands, embarrassed.

The other woman visibly relaxed. "Oh, Clara. I'm so relieved you've brought this up."

"You are?"

"Yes. I...I don't want to hurt Nate's feelings and I know that he was under the control of Coppelius at the time—but the only feelings I have for him are platonic. I mean, he never stopped *talking*."

Clara's mouth dropped open.

"I don't want to be rude," Olympia added hastily. "Don't get me wrong, he's a lovely man... All the things he said, most women would love to hear, despite its..."

"Floweriness?"

"Yes!" Relief softened her expression. "They were lovely sentiments because they were heartfelt, you know, but...they were clearly not meant for me, despite what he thought at the time." She winced.

"What do you mean?"

"It was clear they were meant for someone else. There was too much history in them for them to be about me. I mean, Nate's not for *me*, but whoever those words were for, she's a lucky woman.

Clara didn't know what to say. Her heart pressed against her ribcage. *It's clear they were meant for someone else.*

"Were they for you?" Olympia's expression was innocent.

"Me? What makes you think they were for me?"

She broke into a grin. "You obviously love him. I'm surprised you don't hate me, watching him go through all that for me." Her eyes narrowed. "You *do* love him, don't you?"

Clara sighed. Why deny it? "I do. I always have, ever since we were children. But I don't think he feels the same."

"Why don't you ask him?"

"Because…because I just can't. What if he only loves me as a sister?"

"I don't think you need to worry about that, Clara. I think he loves you as much as you love him. Besides, would you rather live your life always wondering, feeling trapped by it?" She smiled gently. "We're not so different in that respect, except that you're the one trapping yourself."

"What are you, some kind of relationship expert?" Clara grumbled.

Olympia raised an eyebrow. "I've had lots of time to think and watch. And I think you should tell him." She crossed her arms over her chest, decided.

"But what if he—"

"So what if he does? All you've lost then is your fear—"

"And hope."

Olympia made a face. "Fair enough. Look, I know it'll be painful, but I suspect you're a strong woman."

Clara wasn't convinced. She was strong, except when it came to Nate. How could she bear it if he turned away from her?

"Besides, you should do it while you have the chance. Just in case."

"Because life is short?"

"Well, yes. And no. Sometimes it feels very long, so you need to fill it with as much good as you can." She smiled wistfully then her expression darkened. "What will happen to Coppelius?"

"Nothing until the police find him. He disappeared before they arrived."

"Then you need to find him." Olympia leaned forward and put her hand on Clara's knee. "When he and my father were arguing, he was very angry. He threatened Nate's life, and said something about his father, though I didn't understand what it meant."

The concern on Olympia's face made Clara's stomach twist. "Nate believes Coppelius killed his father. But Olympia, the transmissions were coming from you, from your eyes. When Coppelius removed them, Nate said something changed." She patted Olympia's hand. "I don't think he can hurt either of you anymore. The connection was broken."

"Are you sure? That seems too easy. His plan for Nate seemed so...personal."

It was as though Olympia had lit a fuse, and panic ignited in Clara's heart. No, she wasn't sure. She wasn't sure at all. She stood. She had to see Nate, now, and make sure he was all right. "I have to go."

Olympia stood with her, her face flushed. "It's so frustrating. I wish I could help you the way you've helped me...but—"

"Don't worry, Olympia." Clara hugged her with a spontaneity that surprised even her. "You've helped me more than you know. I'll be in touch."

Clara tore the headset off and stalked down the hospital corridor. She was going back to Dreaming Life to speak with Nate, whether he wanted to see her or not. This uncertainty had to end *now*.

TWENTY-TWO

"Come in." Who was it now?

I thought I'd made it clear I wanted to be alone.

Loth had already been to visit that morning, and things between them had been so uncomfortable that Nate had feigned falling asleep. It was a terrible thing to do to your best friend, but he hadn't known what else to do. He just needed the conversation to end and for Loth to go away.

Clara's face peered through the crack in the door. "It's me, Nate."

"Clara, I—" Damn. Loth had told him she was at the hospital. Clara was the *last* person he wanted to see right now. What could he possibly say to her to atone for what he'd done? But he couldn't very well make things even worse by sending her away.

She seemed to know it, too. She cut off his protest by shutting the door gently behind her then stood glancing around self-consciously.

"Sit down, Clara, please." Nate pointed to an armchair near his bed. He might as well get this over with now. Better than sitting here torturing himself with indecision.

She sat awkwardly, perched on the edge. "How are you feeling? You're looking better."

"I'm feeling a bit better, thanks."

She cleared her throat. "The doctor said you've been having headaches?"

Nate nodded. He'd just wanted the damn chips out of his head, all of them, but Ari had explained that it was too dangerous to remove them right now, that his brain might be damaged if they did. He didn't care. He'd rather have damage then be constantly waiting in fear for Coppelius to pull his strings. When the connection between him and Olympia had been broken, he'd been certain it was over. Now, though, he wasn't so sure. He just didn't feel right.

I can't bear it.

"Is there any news about Coppelius?" He tried to keep his voice neutral.

"Not yet. But maybe that means he's gone for good. The police can't seem to find a trace of him, anyway."

"They couldn't find him after he killed my father, either," Nate pointed out.

Clara blushed dully. *Stop being such an ass.* She was trying her best to speak to him, and after everything he'd put her through, he couldn't even give her that. "I'm sorry, Clara, I— How are *you* doing?"

"I'm fine, you know. The usual. Glad to have you back." She grinned, no trace of hurt on her face. "I spoke to Olympia today."

"Oh." The shame tightened its grip around his throat. Another person Coppelius had hurt through him. "How is she?"

"She's good. Great, even, considering the circumstances. She's in the hospital in one of our simulations. She said to say hi."

"Clara, I—"

"Don't worry about that, Nate," she said, as though she'd read his mind. "She doesn't have any feelings for you, and she knows you were under Coppelius's control. She's not upset with you at all. She knows you were as much a casualty as she was."

Not upset? I almost married her against her will. What would've happened if I'd gone through with their plan?

It was too dark a path to go down, not unless he never wanted to come back. "I'm grateful she sees it that way." It was a small consolation.

Silence descended again, and after a few moments, Clara stood and wandered over to the window. "Loth came to see you, right?"

"Yes."

"And?"

"And what? It was awkward. He's...he's not very comfortable around me right now. I can't say I blame him."

"He'll come around. He feels guilty for not being there for you. He feels like he let you down."

He did. But not as badly I let all of you down. "He shouldn't. Nor should my mother." He'd spent several exhausting hours trying to convince his mother that none of this was her fault, though the child inside him wanted to scream otherwise. *"Why didn't you protect me from my own father? How could you not know?"* But they were questions he didn't want the answers to.

"Like I said, they'll get over it. They just need time and to stop worrying about themselves for a few minutes." She winked at Nate, hoping to share the joke.

But Nate couldn't find anything to smile about. And he couldn't pretend to be asleep, not with Clara. *For once in your life, Nate, just face your problems head-on. Otherwise, it's going to tear you—and her—apart.*

"Look, Clara, about what happened—"

"We don't have to do this, Nate. Not now. Not until you're ready."

I'll never be ready for this.

"No, Clara, I need to talk to you. Please, sit down."

Clara returned to her chair. Her smile vanished, replaced by a look of dread, as though she knew what was coming.

And why wouldn't she? She's a smart girl, much smarter than you deserve.

He forced himself to look at her. "Clara, after what happened, I've made a decision. I want to break off our engagement."

She stared at him, stunned. "But I—"

"You probably never thought I meant it, did you? Well, I did, Clara. I meant every word of it. And not because your father was dying." He took a deep breath. *This isn't the way it was supposed to happen.* "I love you, Clara, I always have. Or so I thought. But I can no longer tell what's real. I don't know who I am anymore, or if my feelings for you are real— even if they ever were." He drew his knees to his chest. "I still feel that dark force. No matter what anyone says, The Sandman is still out there. There's nothing to stop him from taking me over again."

He reached convulsively for his eyes then forced his hands into his lap.

"And how much of what happened was even Coppelius? What if I... What if I only thought I've loved you my entire life?" He knotted his hands in the blankets, twisting the fabric around his fingers until they were numb. "I never thought I could ever love anyone but you, Clara, but what if I was wrong?"

"Don't do this, Nate. Please." Tears streamed down Clara's face. "Please, stop."

"Clara, I need you to know this now, how I felt. I should've told you sooner, before this happened, before it changed everything."

"It doesn't have to change anything, Nate. I love you. I—" She bowed her head and tears made damp spots on the fabric of the chair. "Nothing has changed for me. I *still* love you. I'll never love anyone but you. Now we know, and we can be together. Please, Nate."

His body tingled, and his heart rose in his throat as though he were falling from a great height. The moment he'd been waiting for for years, and he was about to smash it—and their hearts—to pieces. "We can't, Clara. Not until I know what's real. I have so many regrets about what happened. I mean, he couldn't have put doubts in my head that weren't already there, could he? And what if it happens again? I couldn't do that to you, Clara. I couldn't live with myself if I hurt you."

"So you're breaking off our engagement to *protect* me?"

"I have to. You're better off without me. You need to find someone else, someone who can take care of you. I have to do this for both our sakes."

"You don't *have* to. When Coppelius was controlling you, you had no choice. Now you do. And you're making the wrong one." She stood and raised her chin. "This isn't logic, Nate. This is just you being Nate, the self-indulgent, spoiled brat you always were. You're choosing for both of us, regardless of how I feel about it. This is one hundred percent for you, not me. Don't insult me by pretending it is."

"Clara—"

"No, Nate. I refuse to sit here and listen to you give up on us. You've loved me your entire life the way I've loved you? You're a liar. If you really loved me, you wouldn't be giving up. I saw how hard you fought, Nate, when Coppelius was manipulating you. And now that you're free from him, that you beat him, you're just giving up."

"Please—"

"No, Nate. I'm not accepting this. We've both been idiotic enough about our feelings for each other. I know you think you're protecting me, but you're not. You may have given up on us, but I haven't. And I won't. We love each other, and it's as simple as that." Her eyes shone, and before Nate could say anything more, she turned and ran from the room.

Nate stared after her. *What have I done?* It hadn't come out the way he'd meant it. He'd only meant to— To what? *You did exactly what you meant to do.* Clara was right. *You are being self-centered, wallowing in your own misery. This didn't just happen to you, Nate. It happened to both of you.*

Her words rang in his ears. *I love you. I have my entire life. Nothing has changed for me. I still love you. I'll never love anyone but you.*

She loved him the way he loved her. She always had. And through his dreams, she'd watched him not only fall in love with another woman, but also grow to hate Clara, to *kill* her.

He loved her. He would've bet his life on it. But what if Coppelius managed to get inside his head again? How long would Clara stand by him as he hurt her, even if he couldn't control it? It *felt* like the monster had gone…but what if he wasn't? It was too much to ask of her, of any person. What if Coppelius twisted his feelings for her? Turned them to hate? Was there a limit to what that bastard could make him do?

Coppelius had taken so much from them, and Nate continued to let him. He'd just thrown away the most important thing in his life—his future with Clara. But he had to stand by his decision until Coppelius was well and truly gone. Nate simply couldn't take the chance, no matter how much it would hurt Clara in the short run. *One day, she'll understand.*

He was just so exhausted by it all. *I've never been so tired in my life.* He lay down and pulled the blankets over his head.

But he couldn't sleep. He hadn't slept for days, once he'd finally woken up. He hadn't told anyone; he didn't want them to worry about him more than they already were, or worse, give him a sedative.

I'm afraid to go to sleep. It seemed like this was to be a day of truth. *I'm terrified. What if he comes to me in my sleep again? What if he—*

His body too exhausted to continue, Nate passed back into the shadows of his own mind as sleep overtook him at last.

TWENTY-THREE

Clara slammed the door to her bedroom so hard it shuddered on its hinges and she resisted the urge to tear it free, kicking and smashing it to smithereens. Instead, she leaned against it and slid to the floor, letting out a string of curses. Normally, she found swearing very satisfying, but today, even turning the air blue didn't help.

I can't believe what just happened. In the space of a few moments, she'd finally gotten everything she'd ever wanted only to have it snatched away, possibly forever.

Nate loves me.

She'd waited so long to hear those words from him, said with all the gravitas of truth, no longer a joke or a tease, but the truth. And he finally had.

And then he'd broken up with her.

After everything she'd done, after everything she'd witnessed, she'd still kept the faith between them, so why hadn't he? She pushed herself to her feet and walked to the bay window. Maybe he was right. Maybe she did deserve better. She'd taken it as self-indulgent twaddle, thinking he'd said it out of fear, but he'd been so certain.

I hate Coppelius. If I ever see him again, I'll murder him. She would gladly spend the rest of her life in prison just to watch him die. To feel his heart stop in her hand.

Ugh.

When had she gotten so violent? The old Nate would've been thrilled with her passion. Maybe if she'd been this way sooner, if she hadn't worried about stupid logic and the consequences of telling him she loved him, he would've said it back, and they would've been together now. He never would've gone away. Coppelius never would've gotten his claws in him.

And Olympia would still be trapped.

It was the one silver lining to losing Nate, the only thing that made Clara's heart any easier.

She turned the conversation over in her mind, dissecting his words. Were they right? Was it possible they only thought they loved each other?

Did she only love him because she'd decided as a child that she did and was too stubborn to change her mind? Just because he was her first love didn't mean he was her true love. Maybe he wasn't even the man she thought he was, or the man she thought he could be.

Maybe she had been blind this entire time to his true nature, to hers. Had she been manipulating what she saw, just as Coppelius had manipulated Nate?

Her love for Nate was the one thing she'd never applied logic to. Maybe she was afraid of the truth. Afraid that if she looked closely and logically enough, she would have to change her mind.

And if she did...what would her life be like without Nate, to not be with him, for it to no longer even be a hope? She could stop waiting. Stop reading into every word he said, every gesture, every expression. Her heart wouldn't break every time another woman's name came up. She would be free. She'd never even considered it before, what it would be like to not be tied to Nate.

For the first time in her adult life, she would be able to have both feet firmly in the future, instead of always having one in the past. Simple and uncomplicated.

And empty.

Nate knew Clara better than anyone else, maybe even better than Loth. Her life was happily and hopelessly entwined with his, and to unravel that... She would be undone, incomplete. To live without Nate would be to live without part of herself. She *could* survive without him, but it would be a miserable existence, a half-life. A life she didn't want.

No, even if Nate was confused, she wasn't. Her feelings for him were real, and she would have to trust that his were as well. Because she wasn't ready to give up. Not now, probably not ever. It was highly illogical, but there it was, and she took a savage delight in it. She would continue to fight for Nate, until he was ready to fight for her.

That settled, Clara turned her mind to the issue of Coppelius. Nate was worried he would come back. That was the other reason he'd given for pushing Clara away.

If they were ever to be happy, they had to get rid of the shadow hanging over them. And to do that, Coppelius had to be gone. Which meant Clara had to find him. But how? And then what? Could it be as easy as handing him over to the police? Would they be able to stop him? Or could she hire someone to make him disappear?

She laughed. What would Loth and Nate think of her right now?

This is exhausting. I'm just running around in circles.

Get some sleep, Clara. You haven't slept properly since Nate came back. Get some sleep and see how things look in the morning.

She was nearly asleep when the alert rang on her transcomm.

Nate was having another dream.

Her stomach twisted. Was this it? Was Coppelius still there, as Nate suspected, making his move? Or would it be another normal dream? There was only one way to find out.

She was just sliding the visor over her eyes when her transcomm went off again.

It could wait. She picked it up to turn off the distracting buzz and caught sight of the caller. George Devereux. The member of the board who oversaw the shares of the company.

Damn. What could he want? It wasn't a call she could ignore.

She glared at the screen as she took the call. "Yes, George? What is it? This isn't a good time."

"I'm so sorry, Clara, but I've had a rather unusual request." His voice was bewildered.

"Request? What do you mean?"

"From Nathanael. I...I normally wouldn't involve you in this, but it's very unusual and—"

The hair on the back of her neck rose. "Just tell me what it is."

"Well, I've just had a call from him, and he's requested that I sign over every single one of his shares to a man named Gordon Vandran."

TWENTY-FOUR

His father looked different than Nate remembered. He was smiling, the lines on his youthful face distinguished rather than weary. The last times Nate had seen his father had been on the day of his death, his features scorched and blackened, and then on the day of his funeral, his face composed and strangely waxen.

He gazed out over the water toward the Dreaming Life tower on the horizon, gleaming in the pink and orange sky of the setting sun. The sea was calm, and yet to Nate's eye, a darkness roiled beneath the still surface, dark, silent shapes gliding through its depths as they waited for the scent of his fear.

Was this another trick? Was the joy that lifted Nate's head, the thankfulness at this chance to see the one who'd shaped his life so completely just another cruelty? A sleight of Coppelius's hand?

Coppelius.

His gratitude at this unexpected gift slipped away as quickly as it had come. This man, the man who was supposed to take care of him, had betrayed him, had opened the door to his mind and let a monster in.

"What are you doing here?" Beyond his father, something broke the surface of the water, tasting the air.

"*Is that how you greet your father, Nathanael?*" But his voice was gentle.

"*You betrayed me. You let Coppelius put something in my head and now he's trying to destroy my life.*" Didn't he understand what he'd done, what he'd cost his son? Ripples lapped at the water's edge.

"*I didn't betray you, Nate. I betrayed him.*"

"*Him? You mean Coppelius?*"

"*Yes. I took his work and claimed it solely as my own. I robbed him of his future.*"

"*That's a lie! You didn't steal anything from him. He wanted to take what you worked so hard for and twist it.*" The ripples grew teeth, scoring the sand.

"*No.*" His father's face hardened. "*That's the lie. He wanted to take Dreaming Life to heights I never could've imagined. But I was jealous and afraid. I thought he would leave me behind, so I acted first and cut him out.*"

"*He killed you.*" Icy water chilled the soles of Nate's feet.

"*My death was an accident, Nathanael, a mistake. You know that.*"

"*You didn't make mistakes. Not like that.*"

"*Regret and shame made me careless, son. Regret is a terrible thing. It eats away at you until you know longer know who you are.*"

Regret and shame. "*Is that what happened to you?*"

"*Yes. And I am sorry, Nathanael, for everything that happened, but there is a way to make it right.*"

"*Make it right? Nothing can change what's happened.*" The water bit at his ankles.

"*No, but it can end it. It can save you.*" His father lifted his chin.

"*I don't need to be saved.*"

His father frowned. "*It can save Clara.*"

"*What do you mean? Is Clara in danger?*" *Something sleek brushed against Nate's leg, curious and curling.*

"*Coppelius will stop at nothing to get what he wants, Nate. Not after what I did to him. If the only way to do that is use Clara, he'll do it.*"

"*What could he do to Clara? She doesn't have one of his damned chips in her head.*"

"*It's not what he'll do to her, Nathanael, it's what he'll make* you *do to her.*"

The sleek thing grew barbs, tender yet, and waiting. "*What do I have to do. I'll do anything.*" As long as it ends.

"*Give Coppelius your shares in Dreaming Life. Give him what's rightfully his. It's a poisoned chalice, and it always will be as long as you have it.*"

"*But then he'll own half the company. I can't do that to Clara and Loth.*" *It would ruin everything. Dreaming Life, their lives.*

"*You would rather stand by and watch their lives destroyed?*"

"*Of course not. I—*"

"*Then do it. And soon. Coppelius isn't a patient man, and this is the only way.*"

"*But—*" *Clara. The barbs hardened, toughening themselves against the world.*

"*Stop whining and do it!*" *For a moment, his father's features wavered. As they solidified again, his mouth was turned down, his eyes pleading.* "*Please, Nate. It's the only way.*" *He began walking toward the deeper water, his legs churning up the surf.*

"*Wait, come back!*" *Nate tried to follow his father, but the barbs pierced the flesh of his legs, impaling him and holding him fast.*" No! Come back. There has to be another way!"

His father strode farther and farther away, the water roiling as it rose over his hips. He turned back when only his face and shoulders remained and regarded Nate.

"Her life is in your hands." Then the water consumed him, and he was gone.

TWENTY-FIVE

"What the hell were you thinking, Nate?"

"Clara—"

"Half the company, Nate. Everything you have!"

"*Clara*—" If he could just get her to listen. But Clara was a force of nature and would listen only when she was ready.

"I thought he couldn't manipulate Nate anymore." Loth was wide-eyed, a steaming mug of coffee clutched in his fingers. Knowing they'd be alerted to what he'd done, Nate had burst into his room and dragged him down the hallway toward Clara's suite. She'd met them halfway, her beautiful face glorious in its anger.

"We all thought that. We thought Olympia's eyes were the only mode of transmission. And we were wrong. So now we have to deal with it." When he'd first woken in a cold sweat, terror had held Nate between its teeth. But as it tightened its grasp, a sudden calm had rushed through his veins, soothing the bite and pushing the fear away. He wasn't going to give in, not this time. It was time for him to fight back. For *everything*.

"So what are we going to do?" Loth took a gulp of coffee, glaring at the sobriety it offered.

Clara yanked on a lock of her hair in frustration. "First thing we need to do is stop the transfer. Then—"

"Both of you stop!" Nate slammed his fist onto the table. "We're going to let him think he won. Let him think my shares are his."

Clara blinked. "What? No, Nate, we can't—"

"Yes, we can. Look, Coppelius hasn't manipulated me into anything. You think I didn't wake up from that dream and realize what was happening? I'm not that stupid."

"Nate, we don't think—"

"It doesn't matter. When I called George and told him to transfer my shares, I knew what I was doing."

"But *why*, Nate?" The anger left her, her shoulders slumping in defeat.

"Because this is the only way we're going to be able to stop Coppelius. I can't live like this anymore. I refuse to. I'm not going to live in fear, with him haunting me. We have to end this."

"But I don't understand. How is giving him your shares going to stop him? You don't actually believe that he'll stop once he gets them, do you?" She held out her hands, imploring him.

"Of course not. He'll take mine then he'll come after the two of you. So we need to stop him now."

Loth frowned. "But—"

"I have a plan."

"Okay, but—" He placed his coffee on Clara's night table and took a deep breath.

"Shut up, Loth." Clara's shoulders had straightened and her eyes gleamed. "Nate, what's your plan?"

"It's going to take some time to get the shares transferred over. I told George that there was no rush, to take his time. And that during that time, I can simply change my mind and have the shares reverted back to me with a single phone call."

"Then how is Coppelius going to think he's won?" Clara's teeth toyed with her bottom lip.

"He won't. Everything he wants is just within his reach but can be snatched back at any time. It's going to make him crazy."

"So that's your plan? Antagonize him? Nate, you have no idea what he'll try to do to you!" Clara crossed her arms over her chest. He'd better hurry, or she was going to put her foot down.

"He'll try to kill me."

"*What?* And—"

"It's the only way. He's going to have to make his move. If he's still transmitting to me, he has to be somewhere close, right?"

"Yes, but—" Her eyes narrowed. The foot was coming down.

"So we use me as bait, draw him out of hiding or goad him into making a mistake. Then we catch him and turn him over to the police."

But it was Loth whose foot came down first. "You can't use yourself as bait. What if—"

"What? Loth, I don't like it either, but what choice do we have? Live every minute wondering what he's going to do next?" Nate couldn't look at them. "Loth, he…he threatened to go after Clara."

"He *what?*" Clara's voice was brittle.

"Don't be scared, Clara. We'll—"

"I'm not scared, Nate. I'm pissed off. How dare he try to manipulate you by threatening me?"

Clara. *His* Clara. His heart swelled with pride.

"He'll do whatever it takes. I think what he did to Olympia proves that."

"Which is exactly why this whole plan is so mad. No way. Clara? Are you going to back me up here?"

Loth's frantic expression volleyed between the two of them. Nate couldn't blame him. The situation was dire if Loth had to be the sensible one.

Clara thought for a moment then nodded. "I think we should do it."

"You *do*?"

"Yes. Nate's right. We can't sit back and do nothing, waiting for the other shoe to drop. I don't like it, at all. But I trust Nate." She squeezed his hand and smiled. "And if he feels this is the only way, then we'll do it." She grabbed Loth's hand as well.

Loth looked at them both like they'd lost their minds. *And maybe we have.* "So how are we going to stop him?"

Clara tapped her chin. "Every time he transmits to Nate, Ari gets more information about the signal, but since he bounces it off different satellites each time, his location is constantly changing. Tracking him down is going to be difficult." She began pacing, and hope rose in Nate. This was Clara at her best. Analyzing a problem and finding the solution. "Drawing him out is our best bet. We originally thought he might be able to damage Nate's brain simply because we didn't really know the nature of the transmissions or what his plans were. Now we know the signal isn't strong enough for him to do more than manipulate Nate's mind, and then it's mostly through his dreams." She turned to them. "If he's desperate, he's going to try to increase that influence any way he can."

"Can't we just drug Nate up so that Coppelius can't transmit to him then force him to come looking? There's no way he could get into Dreaming Life undetected." Loth perched on the edge of Clara's bed.

Nate sat next to him, their shoulders touching. "No. I refuse to constantly be on the defensive. Besides, he's probably too much of a coward to put himself out there like that. I want to force his hand. Now. I'm going to take just enough of a sleeping shot to get me under. From what I know about him, he's going to keep manipulating me though my dreams."

"Then what?"

"Then we'll have to see. I don't think he cares exactly what happens to me—prison, death, whatever—as long as he gets his shares."

"So what can we do? What if he tries to make you hurt yourself—or someone else?" Loth avoided looking at Clara.

"Clara, do you still have access to my dreams?"

"Yes." She blushed. "I know I should have—"

"No, I'm glad you do. You're going to have to monitor them. If things start getting really bad, you tell Loth, and he'll either wake me up, or knock me out. Agreed?"

"Okay. We need to take anything out of your room that you could use to hurt yourself—or Loth."

"Yes. And we need to keep this quiet. If this gets out to the public...well, you know what it'll do to our reputation. So just the three of us, yes?"

"And Ari." Clara's voice was firm.

"Arienne? Really? That strange researcher who looks like a ghost?" *What have I missed?*

Clara put her hands on her hips. "Yes, Nate. We're going to need her. She's helped us get this far."

"And you're sure we can trust her?"

"Definitely." Clara thrust out her chin, just the way she'd done when they were children. There would be no arguing with her.

"Okay then. I'm happy with that."

"Right, well, I guess I'd better go and clear my schedule." Loth's didn't seem convinced, his expression still unsure.

"Me too. I'll also go and tell Ari the plan." Now that they had a plan, she was all action. Just as he'd known she would be.

"Clara, wait." He held out a hand to her.

She took a seat next to him. "You're not have second thoughts, are you?"

"About Coppelius? No. But about what I said to you before—" He tightened his fingers around hers.

"Nate, we don't have to talk about that now. Just... Let's wait until this is over and you have a chance to really think about things without the shadow of Coppelius hanging over you."

"No, I'm sorry, Clara. I didn't mean what I said. You were right, I was being selfish, and a coward." He turned her hand over and rubbed his thumb over her palm.

She relaxed against him. "You weren't *all* wrong, Nate. I think we've both been living under these ideas for so long that we never had a chance to step back and look at them for what they truly are." She rubbed her cheek on his shoulder. "I'm not going to lie, I was devastated when you said those things to me. But now that I've had a chance to think about it—"

"You've decided you're better off without me."

She pulled back and looked up at him. "Nate, I want you more than I ever have. I always wondered whether or not you cared for me as more than a sister, a friend—"

"I do, Clara, I always have." *We were both so stupid.*

"I know that now, Nate. I saw how hard you fought when Coppelius was manipulating you. I felt your love for me slipping through his stranglehold. I *felt* it. I know why you said those things, Nate, and I'm glad you did. It's time for us to grow up and *choose* this."

"I will always choose you, Clara. I should've told you sooner, but I thought... I didn't think you thought I was good enough, that your love for me was just another obligation. I did so many stupid things trying to get your attention....and now that I finally have it, I might lose everything."

"We are not going to lose, Nate. Not now that we have everything to fight for."

He grasped her chin gently in his fingers. "I love you, Clara."

"I love you too, Nate. I—"

He pressed his lips to hers. They would have this moment, Coppelius be damned. The years of waiting in uncertainty, the fear and the grief that had been so entwined with anything good in their lives...no matter what happened next, they would have this kiss, *their* kiss, at last. Here, in the heart of their castle, of the kingdom they would die to defend.

They lived in their moment for as long as they could, and Nate could scarcely believe being with Clara was no longer a dream. But like all dreams, it was fleeting.

But I don't mind, because what we have will last forever.

At least, it would if they had anything to say about it.

Reluctantly, Nate broke the kiss and stood, his fingers still linked with Clara's. He looked down at her with a grim smile. "Let's go save our empire."

TWENTY-SIX

Clara stared at the screen, willing something, anything to happen. What was taking Coppelius so long? It had been two days.

The alert pinged. *Finally.* Nate was having a dream. His dreams in the last couple days had been little more than fractured images, wisps of the mundane. Was that Coppelius's plan? Lull them into a false sense of security then pounce? Well, Clara would be waiting for him, no matter how many irrelevant conversations and mundane tasks she had to wade through.

She took a deep breath and slid on her headset. Was this going to be another false alarm?

Clara was in a field. It was the apex of night, and the sky sparkled with stars against a great black abyss. A gray mist rose from the cold, damp grass at her feet, adorning the flowing fabric of her dress with a silver lace and chilling her skin. Nate surrounded her, his sleeping mind confused and tired. So very, very tired. So unlike the waking man. His vulnerability chilled Clara more than the mist. He can do this.

The fog swirled and twisted, and out of it rode a man on a pale horse, its hooves silent over the ground. For a moment, it seemed as though it would pass Nate by, but then it stopped, and the rider peered down at her from out of the gloom.

Coppelius.

He wore black, and his face was ghostly and drawn.

"What are you doing here, Coppelius?" Nate's voice was soft, broken. Only Clara could sense the strength beneath his words. "You've already taken everything from me. Clara. My legacy." Good, even in his dream, even as exposed as he was, Nate kept to the plan.

"You think you're so clever, don't you?" Coppelius leered down at him, his mouth stretched impossibly wide. "But you'll never win."

Fatigue suddenly swamped Clara, not the normal craving for sleep, but the exhaustion of merely existing. What was happening? Fight, Nate, keep fighting.

"Your time is done, Nathanael."

"I'm so tired." His mind held an alarming truth. He was *tired.* Maybe this was a mistake.

"I know. It's time for you to go. You don't need to fight it."

Why would he fight it? He had no reason to stay. He'd given away his legacy. His mother would never forgive him. Clara and Loth hated him. He hated himself. He'd failed them all, so many times. He was no better than his father, doomed to the same fate. Cursed.

Inside him, Clara's temper reared its head. Coppelius was making his move. And he was too strong.

"There's a dark force inside me. I can feel it." Nate's voice held surrender. He was still fighting, wasn't he?

"Of course there is, Nate. We all have a darkness inside us." Coppelius grinned, his teeth wolfish in the starlight.

"I can't overcome it."

Coppelius stroked the horse's mane. *"You don't need to overcome it, Nathanael. You need to embrace it. How do you think you'll feel when you embrace it?"*

"Free." Again, it rang true.

"Acceptance is not the same as giving up, Nathanael."

"I know, but—"

He was so exhausted, so forlorn that Clara wanted to burst into tears. She was going to find Coppelius and wring his neck with her bare hands.

Nate finally gave Coppelius a small smile. *"Tell me what I need to do."* Here it comes. Now we'll find out his plan.

"Just let me in, Nathanael."

"As if I could stop you." Clara held her breath.

It was a risky strategy, but Nate was safe in the Dreaming Life tower, Loth at his side. *I still don't like this.* Even though she'd agreed to it, now that it was happening, she wished she could knock the Sandman off his horse.

The horse pawed the ground and tossed its head.

"So I have to embrace the darkness?"

"Yes, Nate, that's the only way to end it."

Stop speaking in riddles, both of you. What's the plan? Impatience gnawed at Clara. She just wanted to figure it out so they could get this over with.

"End it." Hollowness swallowed Nate's heart, a sudden screaming void that took Clara's breath away. No. What was happening?

Coppelius dismounted and walked away into the fog, leading the horse and Nate behind him.

They came to a stop on the edge of a tower. Nate stared down into the ocean of fog, the void inside him now a whimper. "Clara once told me to accept it. She was right. She always is."

"Yes. Go on, Nathanael, listen to Clara." He pointed to the edge. This was what Coppelius wanted. Nate's death.

Without preamble, Nate obliged, stepping off the edge, mist slipping through his fingers like a ghost.

As they plummeted down, their screams lost forever in the fog, a single sound carried over the rushing in their ears.

Coppelius laughed.

TWENTY-SEVEN

"Answer, damn you!" Loth's transcomm continued to ring, until finally, just as Clara was about to hurl hers against the wall and sprint to Nate's room, he answered.

"Yes?" His voice sounded blurry.

"Have you been *sleeping*? You're supposed to be keeping an eye on Nate!" After she'd witnessed Nate's dream, she'd dispatched Loth to his quarters, to stand guard in the living room attached to Nate's bedroom. If Nate tried to leave, to follow the instructions Coppelius had given him, he would have to go through Loth first.

Which might be a lot easier than I anticipated. One job, Loth. That's all.

"No, of course not. I mean, I may have dozed off a bit, but—"

She spoke through gritted teeth. "Go see if Nate is still in his room. Now."

"Clara, he's fine. I don't—"

"*Now.*"

"Fine." He grumbled under his breath at her as he crossed the room to Nate's bedroom door. "Nate? You okay?" There was no answer. "Nate?"

"Open the door."

"Clara, what's gotten into you?"

"There was another dream, and I think Coppelius is trying to make his move. He wants Nate to hurt himself. Please, Loth, just check."

The whoosh of a door opening came through the comm. "He's in bed, asleep."

"Make sure it's really him."

"What? Who else would it be?"

"Oh my god, Loth, are you serious? Do you know you? Remember when you and Nate used to sneak out when you were kids? What did you put in your bed to fool Mom and Dad?"

"Good point. Hang on."

Clara held her breath for the few seconds Loth was gone.

"Nope, it's definitely him. And he's getting a bit ripe, I might add. When he wakes up, I'll try to get him to have a shower."

Relief washed over Clara. *He's still here, safe.* But it had been a close call. "Good. I'm going to talk to Ari, see if she managed to get anything from that transmission. If so, we can go after him."

"Okay. Just...don't go too overboard."

"Overboard? What does *that* mean?"

"Well, I hate to say this, Clara, but when it comes to Nate, you can be a bit...irrational. I'm just saying."

"Thanks for the help, Loth." He was talking nonsense, but Clara was in no mood to argue. She had a Sandman to hunt.

***

Clara balanced on a wooden chair in Ari's office. It was the most uncomfortable chair in the world—hard, with thin fabric stretched over completely unnecessary angles. "Are your chairs this uncomfortable on purpose?"

Ari grinned. "Of course. Don't want people getting too comfortable and, you know, coming to *talk* to me." She winked.

"I'm going to have to try that." Loth often spent the entire day on the couch in Clara's office, moaning about whatever trivial matter was ruining his life. "So, what have you found out?"

"Still nothing. He's like a damn ghost. The minute I think I have him, he's gone again."

Clara's heart sank. "But— We need to do something. Nate's all right for now, but Coppelius is trying his best to get to him. He wants this over." She related Nate's last dream to Ari.

"I'm so sorry that you had to witness that, Miss Clara." She put her hand on Clara's shoulder. "But you can't dwell on that now. What's done is done. We just have to deal with it."

"But I thought you said there were no options."

"There aren't, really. At least, not for Nate. But I might have something for *you*."

"Let me hear it. Whatever it is, it has to be better than just sitting around waiting for Coppelius to strike."

"Okay, but I have to be clear: this is in the experimental phase only. I still need to run a bunch of tests before we can even begin to think about using it." She raised her eyebrows at Clara's obvious disappointment.

"I mean it, Clara." For once she dropped the title. "This is dangerous—and at the moment, highly illegal—tech. I probably shouldn't even be telling you about it, but...well, I'll never forget what that bastard did to Nate's father. This is for him as well."

She guided Clara over to her bookshelf. "You can't tell anyone about this, ever. Do you promise?"

"I promise."

Ari stared at her for a moment then nodded. "Okay. This is the program Coppelius wanted from Nate's father. It was the last missing piece of his plan. If you ask me, I think it's why Coppelius might have killed him. If he'd gotten his hands on this..."

"What is it?"

"It's similar to the program Coppelius is using to manipulate Nate. Only it tricks the brain to a much greater extent. It was intended for Dreaming Life, to act as a patient-driven therapy. It uses haptic technology to convince the patient's nervous systems that they *are* healing, which in turn prompts their bodies to commit almost super-human acts of regeneration. The mind is an incredibly powerful thing."

"Don't I know it."

Ari gave her a grim smile. "But it can also go the opposite way, and this is what Nate's father suspected Coppelius wanted to do with it. It can also trick the brain into *hurting* its host."

"You mean you could injure, and perhaps even kill, people from a distance, without ever touching them?"

"Yes. Now you understand why Nate's father didn't want Coppelius to get his hands on it. He patented it a million ways, encrypted it...anything to keep Coppelius from getting any part of it that could be used to formulate the rest. If he'd been a different kind of man...well, he could've sold it for a fortune into the wrong hands. Even in the right hands, it's a terrible thing. That's why we never did anything with it. Only four people knew it even existed, and two of them are dead. And now, you know."

"So what are we waiting for?"

"Clara, like I said, it still needs a lot of testing. I'm going to start running some trials now, so that when Coppelius strikes next, we might be able to use it. He has to be within a reasonable distance in order to affect Nate—"

"But he *is*. That means he's already somewhere here in the city."

"Yes. But we can track him when Nate's having a dream. The manipulation is only half of it. We still have to find out where he's hiding."

"Then it's useless. He's a coward. He's never going to show his face."

"Are you sure about that? Don't underestimate the desire for revenge, Clara. If Coppelius is planning to make Nate hurt himself, the way he did in the dream, I have a feeling he's the type of man who'll want to watch it to the end. He's twisted like that."

"Let's get started with the testing then." Clara was full of nervous energy but at least now she had somewhere to direct it, somewhere she was comfortable. The laboratory was her house. She could finally do something to help Nate rather than sitting around feeling useless. "Should—" Her transcomm sounded.

Loth.

What now? He probably wanted to take a break. That was fair enough. But he could wait, just an hour.

"Loth, look, I'll take over in a bit okay? Ari and I—"

"He's gone." There was a hysterical note to Loth's voice. "He's gone."

"Nate? What do you mean? You were supposed to be watching him!"

"I know, Clara. Damnit. Don't you think I know that?"

"Then what happened?"

"I— I must've fallen asleep—"

"Loth—"

"I know! I went to see if I could haul him into the shower, but he was gone. I've already called down to security—"

"Well, at least you managed to do something sensible. For once." Seriously, how could her brother run a billion-dollar corporation but not be able to keep track of a sleeping man?

"*All right*, Clara. I feel bad enough. Anyway, they've got footage of him leaving the Dreaming Life building. I'm on my way after him now. He was heading toward the downtown core."

What was he doing? Even though he was awake and should be fine, Clara didn't like it. "Fine, keep in touch. Find him, Loth. Keep him safe."

"I will... Clara, there was something else."

"What?" Could this get any worse?

"There's something strange about him in the footage. He...he looks like he's asleep. I think he's sleepwalking. That sleeping draught? The syringe is empty."

Sleepwalking. Coppelius was making his move now. "But that should've knocked him out too much for Coppelius to affect him!" No, no, no. There were lots of tall buildings downtown.

"Yeah, well it didn't."

That meant Nate would be a puppet under Coppelius's control, without enough consciousness to fight back. She hung up on her brother. It had gone beyond a dream now—Coppelius could manipulate him at will. *We've delivered him right into Coppelius's hands.* "Ari, we don't have time for experiments. Coppelius is going to try to kill Nate, now. He's gotten him out of Dreaming Life, and he's—"

"But Clara, it's too—"

"We don't have a choice! This is our only chance. What if Loth doesn't catch up to him in time? What if he— Please, Ari, please. I don't care what can go wrong. I want to take the risk. I *need* to."

"But it isn't logical—"

"To hell with logical! I love him, Ari. I can't lose him, not like this. We're supposed to…supposed to—" She could no longer speak, could no longer breathe. Nate was going to die and there was nothing she could do. By the time they'd explained everything to the authorities, it would be too late.

"Ari, *please.*"

The older woman gazed at her, her indecision clear. Then she threw up her hands. "You're right. This is no time for logic." She reached up and took a small oblong case off the shelf. "Here, sit down." Clara sat on the edge of a chair while Ari pulled a thin, delicate-looking visor from the box and hesitated, as though she was still unsure. "Clara—" But at the look on Clara's face, she relented. "This visor has everything you need. You'll be able to communicate with me, and I can communicate with Loth. I'll let him know what's happening once you're on your way." She put her hand on Clara's arm. "Please, be careful."

Clara took the visor and turned it over in her hands. "I will be. And I understand the risk. If anything happens to either of us, it's not your fault, Ari."

"I'll keep that in mind while I'm rotting away in prison," Ari grumbled as she quickly set up the equipment. "Okay, are you ready?"

Clara nodded. "Do I need to put the visor on now?"

"No, when you find Coppelius. Just keep your transcomm on and I'll tell you where Nate goes."

"How can you even do that?" Who the hell was Ari?

"I'll be using the data-collection sensors all over the city to track the Dreaming Life chip in Nate's head." Her nostrils flared. "Really, Clara, it's not that complicated."

I just have to trust her. "Let's go."

"Now remember, in order for the program to work, you really have to be sure about what you're imagining, be it handcuffs, or whatever. The more you believe it, the more his body will too. And you have to be within eyesight of him—the range isn't that far on the prototype. With any luck, you'll be able to keep him immobile until the police—who I shall be notifying ASAP—get there."

"Ari, you've got this all planned out, don't you?"

"Are you kidding? Just because this technology has terrible potential doesn't mean I abandoned it. I still believe there's a use for it, in the right hands."

"Well, I'm not sure if this counts, but I'm grateful."

Ari reached over and gave Clara a hug, ignoring her look of surprise. "Good luck."

TWENTY-EIGHT

The streets of Portfade stretched out before Clara. Her heart beat painfully in her chest as she craned her neck, searching for any sign of Nate. All around her, people strolled down the street with not a care in the world, oblivious to her panic. *How long has it been since I've been out in the real world?* Aside from her run to Draglight, she couldn't remember the last time she'd left the Dreaming Life tower. It was surreal, a dreamscape of its own.

You're not dreaming, Clara, not this time.

"I'm on the street. Any eyes on Nate?" She clutched the visor in her hand, its smooth edges anchoring the last shred of her self-control.

Ari's voice came from far away, echoing slightly. "Yes. Loth's right behind him. I've told him to just keep his distance and not do anything until we find Coppelius."

"Hopefully, he'll do a better job than he did before."

"He will. He's very upset, Clara. Go easy on him."

"When did you get so diplomatic, Ari?"

She snorted. "Okay, Loth says he's still heading downtown. There's apparently some kind of event going on. Meteor shower. There's a big crowd, fireworks, that sort of thing."

Of course, the meteor shower. Clara had forgotten in all the commotion. "The perfect opportunity for Nate to get lost in the crowd and for some kind of accident to happen."

"I agree. Coppelius has timed it perfectly."

"Do you really think he's going to be there?"

"Yes. That sadistic bastard isn't going to let Nate slip through his fingers. He'll want to make sure all the loose ends are tied up."

Clara zigzagged through the streets, which were increasingly filling with people.

Damn it, since when did all these people care about rocks in space?

She darted between couples and families, her progress frustratingly slow. When she finally crashed into a young couple—a tall man clutching tightly to the hand of a petite, dark-haired synadroid—she stopped. This wasn't going to work.

Clara, you idiot. Think. This is your *city. You grew up in this grid.*

Annoyed with herself, she darted down an empty side street.

That's better.

By the time she made it to the pedestrian-only zone in the center of downtown, it was full of spectators coming to watch the meteors. People were heading toward the large central graveyard—the only hills in Portfade and the best vantage points from which to see the coming show—chatting excitedly and occasionally pausing to peer up at the sky in anticipation. Vendors called out as they walked past, offering samples and specials, and Clara's mouth watered. It had been hours since she'd last eaten.

How can you even think of food right now?

But that *smell*. The nostalgia was overwhelming. She and Nate had often come to these sightings. They'd been one of Clara's favorite things as a teenager. She'd looked to the sky then, believing that was where her future lay, not in a laboratory. Nate had been bored by it all. And yet, every time Clara went, he tagged along, all the while making sure she knew how dull he found it. She'd always wondered why he'd bothered to come.

Because he loves you.

The last time had been nearly ten years ago, the day after her father's funeral. The day after they'd been betrothed. They'd skipped out on the celebrations on the cemetery lawn just before midnight and instead climbed the bell tower, an old relic that Clara loved. They'd broken in as usual, carefully lifting the old rotting boards out of the way. Clara always expected the inside to be as decrepit as the outside, but it was forever neatly swept, as though someone knew it was their special place and was trying to keep house for them. Out of respect for that kindness, Clara always replaced the boards carefully, just in case.

They'd climbed all the way up to the belfry, Clara still in her mourning clothes, where they could stand at the wide, arched windows and look out over the entire city, watching the lights and listening to the urban noises all around them. As usual, their gazes were drawn to the Dreaming Life tower, the tallest building in Portfade—probably in all of Foxwept. It gleamed, a soaring fortress of glass and steel that reached for the stars. It was the closest she was ever going to get to them, now that her father was dead. She wouldn't change a thing now, of course, but back then, the dream of space had seemed like the most important thing in the world. Perhaps she would find a new star or planet, and name it after Nate. None of the other girls he knew could do that for him.

"How are you doing?" Nate had leaned with one elbow on the railing as he'd asked her, and she'd resisted the urge to chastise him for being reckless.

If anyone else had asked her that question, she would've snapped at them, would've demanded to know how the hell they thought she felt? Both her parents were dead. All she had left in the world were her twin brother and this boy standing before her, a beloved boy on whom she'd hung all her hopes for the future.

Her life with Nate had always been full of this bitter sweetness. Perhaps that was why it felt so real to her, more than if he'd simply fallen at her feet and professed his undying devotion.

She could see now he'd been doing that the entire time, just in his own way, just as she had. They'd been telling each other in little ways all their lives, but she'd been asleep to it until now, caught in a dream of what true love should be, a non-messy, perfect dream. A lie.

"I'm okay."

He'd known it wasn't the truth and had taken her hand as they stood watching in silence as the meteors passed overhead, bright and fast as shooting stars. Even though it meant nothing, Clara made a wish.

When the last trail had died off, she lifted her face to Nate's. "What are we going to do now?" She had meant all of them—her, Nate, and Loth—but Nate had misunderstood, or at least pretended to.

"I don't know, Clara. All I know is that I'm going to be your husband. Beyond that, nothing matters. I know we're only fifteen, but I'm going to take care of you, you'll see. I won't let you down. I promise to make all your dreams come true."

Fireworks exploded over their heads and in her chest in every color of the rainbow, and the cheers that rose from the crowd carried all the way out to the tower, as though they'd heard Nate's declaration and shared Clara's heart. When the last firework died down, Nate had turned toward her, and for a moment, she'd thought he was going to kiss her. Her first kiss, her first love. Half of her hoped he would—it was the only thing short of resurrection that could salve her broken heart—and yet part of her dreaded it, knowing that the pain of the moment would be forever intertwined with the pleasure.

And who knew how different their lives would've been if Loth hadn't staggered drunkenly up the stairs, the wooden railings groaning a warning as he crashed back and forth, shouting out their names.

They'd broken apart, self-conscious, and never again had Nate spoken to her about love, unless she counted his joking—which she didn't. *But it was you who decided he was teasing, Clara. You who told him he wasn't serious.* Had she pushed him away the entire time, unknowingly? Well, never again. Whatever happened tonight, she was going to make it clear to Nate every single day how she felt about him, the good and the bad.

She just had to catch Coppelius first.

"Ari? Is Loth still following Nate?"

"Yes. He lost him for a moment, but he's got him again. Where are you?"

"I'm almost at the cemetery. There must be hundreds of people here." Clara thanked the universe she was tall.

"Thousands, I would wager, if the news reports are anything to go by."

Thousands. How would she find Coppelius in that many people?

Keep talking to Ari. Wherever Nate is going, that's where Coppelius is going to be.

"Ari? Where's Nate now?"

"Loth said he's heading toward the graveyard, following the crowd."

What did Coppelius have planned? Did he mean to kill Nate then just slip away into the crowd? Surely he knew that Nate's murder would open a huge investigation. After everything that had happened with Olympia, he had to know he would be the number one suspect. He'd managed to escape before, but not now, not when people were already looking for him.

Ari's voice crackled. "He's lost him, Clara."

"What? Ari? Like, *lost*-lost?"

"Yes." Panic edged the older woman's voice. "In the crowd."

"Damn it, Loth." Though Clara couldn't blame him. Even she was finding it nearly impossible to see anything but a blur of faces and bodies, pale and ghostly in the eerie light from the candles and transcomms.

Where the hell could Nate be going? Why would Coppelius bring him here? It wasn't like he could just kill him in front of everyone, could he? How would he even—

Her heart seemed to stop mid beat.

He stepped off the edge, mist slipping through his fingers like a ghost.

The bell tower.

Did Coppelius know that the tower had special meaning to Clara? Was it the last twist of his knife? Here, at one of the largest celebrations in Portfade, his death would be public, the suicide of one of

Foxwept's most prominent young elites. The media would eat it up, a PR nightmare that could destroy the empire their families had built, *especially* if it was leaked that somehow their technology was involved. He was a devil, she had to give him that.

But so am I. The darkness she had told Nate lived inside all of them woke up.

"Ari, tell Loth to go to the bell tower. Nate is going to try to jump. He—"

"He says he has no idea how to get in."

Of course he wouldn't remember. "Tell him to go around the back. There'll be a couple of loose boards. He needs to pry them off and go up the stairs. And tell him to hurry."

"Done. He's heading there now. Any sign of Coppelius?"

"Not yet, I—"

But there he was.

He stood ten yards back from the tower, his face tipped toward the sky. The crowd's backs were to him, their eyes on the stars as the very first of the meteorites passed overhead.

Clara slipped on the visor. The world became covered with a faint gray film, as though some of the color had been leached from it—except for the sky, which seethed crimson. Did anyone notice her? Of course they didn't. The darkness in Clara laughed. Coppelius had picked the perfect time for his plan— for Clara. All around her, people wore visors to record the spectacle. No one even glanced her way.

She tapped Coppelius on the shoulder and spoke into his ear. "You can't have him."

Coppelius turned, his eyes wide in his ghostly face and his mouth twisted into an ugly sneer. "What are you doing here? Come to watch the show?"

"I've come to watch your end, Sandman."

He laughed, a horrible rasping sound that made Clara's teeth hurt. "You're delusional, child. What do you plan to do? Have me arrested?" He peered over her shoulder. "No one is paying us any attention, my dear."

"I don't need them to pay any attention." It took every ounce of willpower she had to keep her eyes on Coppelius and not glance up at the tower. *Hurry, Loth.* "I'm going to take care of you myself."

"Oh yes? And how do you plan to do that?"

She ignored his question. "Did you really think you would get away with it?"

"Yes. But then I didn't account for you, did I? Is that what you want to hear? Fine, you almost caught me. But it's gone too far now. Soon, this will all be over, and I'll disappear, like a bad dream." He looked at Clara appraisingly. "You could do better than him, you know."

"Better than Nate?"

"He's weak, like his father. I barely had to turn his head before he tossed you aside for a woman who can't even speak!" He chortled, clearly amused with himself. "And yet here you are, still trying to save him. Have you got no pride?"

Clara didn't have the patience for doubt right now. "I saw how hard he fought you, Coppelius. If you think you can convince me that Nate doesn't love me, you're so very wrong. Try again."

His surprise was almost comical. "You saw— How?"

Clara snorted. "When you go into a dream, you come into my house. And you weren't invited. Let Nate go, now." Her voice held an easy strength she didn't feel.

"It doesn't matter anyway. It will soon be over."

"How could you do this to him? Nate never did anything to you."

"Really? Is that what you think? His father robbed me, robbed Foxwept of what was rightfully ours. Any hint of war could've been avoided. Dreaming Life would've been the most powerful corporation, Foxwept the most powerful province in one of the strongest nations in the world. And his father threw it all away over one boy."

"*His* boy."

Coppelius dismissed Nate with a wave of his hand. "We all have to make sacrifices, my dear." He looked at her sharply. "You know that as much as anyone."

"I'm done making sacrifices. I'm ready to take them."

The sky filled with light as fireworks were released all around them, the high-pitched whining as the rockets cleared the crowd before bursting into multi-colored showers of light a song in Clara's ears. All around them, the crowd gasped, their upturned faces bathed in radiance.

It merely made Coppelius's features more ghoulish. "Almost, dear. You're almost done. Just one more." He pointed to the top of the tower.

The next illumination of fireworks showed two men grappling with each other on the balcony in front of the bell.

Nate and Loth. And Loth was going to lose. He'd always fought with charm, not fists. And after what Nate had done to Spalazani...

She was running out of time.

"This is the last chance I'll give you, Coppelius. Stop this now. Stop Nate from jumping."

"No."

Ari whispered in her ear, Clara's battle cry. "You're connected." Her hands tingled as the visor initiated. *Time to stop him, now.* To hold him, to keep him in check.

Or maybe something more. *Whatever you choose, make sure you believe it.* She closed her eyes and willed the means to stop him into being.

A familiar sword appeared in Clara's hand, platinum with a ruby-studded hilt. The ridges of the wrapped hilt felt so real under her fingers and her arm strained under the perceived weight. *Amazing.* A sword wasn't what she'd intended, but Coppelius had threatened Nate, had threatened her heart. And so it was her heart that chose.

Coppelius stared at the sword, confusion spreading across his face. He glanced around. Surely someone else could see the woman standing before him, a shining blade in her hand?

But the crowd was focused on the fireworks, their eyes still on the sky and their voices raised in wonder. Even if they were to turn and look, all they would see was a young woman speaking to an older man.

As he stared at the crowd in disbelief, Clara pressed her advantage, took a few running steps, and ran the sword through Coppelius's traitorous heart.

It went through him so easily, the steel tempered by everything in her soul. His back arched as the chip in his brain told his nervous system he'd been run through. He and Clara stood face to face, nearly touching, as his gaze traveled down her arm to where the hilt protruded from his chest. He grabbed at her arms, his face whitening as his hands refused to hold her.

"It's not— It's not possible." He clawed at the collar of his shirt, as though loosening it could make a difference.

"Maybe not. But your brain thinks it is." She smiled at him. "Do you know how weak the flesh is, Sandman, compared to the power of the mind?" She laughed. "But of course you do. It was the only way you could ever control Nate—by poisoning his mind. A coward's weapon."

He tried to snarl at her, one last act of bravado as his heart failed him. "I'll—"

"Die a broken man, unknown. A sad old man whose last breath was nothing more than a whisper."

Coppelius sank to his knees, one hand outstretched for her.

"No one will ever mourn you, or even know of your passing. You will be erased, and fade away like every nightmare eventually does."

He lay on the ground, his breath hitching in his chest, and his. eyes rolling wildly in their sockets. as though they were struggling to wake from a bad dream. With an anguished cry, he pressed his fingers over them.

"Shh." Clara knelt beside him and pulled his hands away. "Close your eyes, Sandman. It's time to sleep." She ran her hand over his eyes, closing them. "Sleep."

And finally, he did, his last breath leaving his body just as Nate's hit the ground.

EPILOGUE

"It's nearly time to go. Are you ready?" Clara brushed her lips over Nate's forehead, and he grinned at her, reaching up to hold her there.

"You look beautiful, Clara."

She laughed gently. It was good to see him relaxed enough to joke. His health was coming back, slowly, but it was never his body that she worried about.

"How would you know? I could be wearing one of your mother's dresses right now."

Nate grinned. "You're wearing that green dress, the one with the gold foil birds printed on it."

"How could you possibly know that?" Despite being blind, Nate could always tell what she was wearing.

"I remember the way it feels between my fingers. The way it fastens at your throat with the tiny gold buttons." He crept his fingers up the hem of her neckline, and she leaned into his touch, before bringing his fingers to her lips and kissing them.

"Well, you're right. As you always are, these days."

"It only took losing my sight to finally win an argument, eh?"

She glanced at him sharply, searching for self-pity or resentment in his face, anything that would let her know he wasn't as content as he led her to believe.

But there was none. This Nate, relaxed and at peace with everything in his world, was real.

"Should we cancel?" The thought of taking Nate back to their room and slowly undressing him as he traced every inch of her body was much more appealing.

He smiled again. "I would love nothing more. But we promised. It's not like you to break a promise, Clara."

"When did you get reasonable?" she grumbled.

"Ever since my mind became my own again." His smile stayed, but Clara cupped the side of his face in sympathy.

Although Nate's body would heal over time, his mind would always bear the scars of what Coppelius had done to him. But at least he was alive. The surgeon at the hospital had said that if he hadn't been asleep when he'd jumped, if the ground had been concrete rather than soft soil and thick grass, he'd never have survived the six-story fall. Even so, it was a miracle.

But he *had* survived, and that was the important thing. Clara had to keep reminding herself, every time the thought of what could've happened came to her, in that vulnerable moment right before sleep.

She'd expected to have nightmares about it for the rest of her life. About the ease with which her sword had pushed through the Sandman's heart. The savage joy that had gone through hers when she'd done it. The sound of Nate's body breaking as he fell beside her, his strings cut at last. The last gasp from Coppelius, somewhere between a curse and a laugh.

But her dreams remained quiet, as though they'd retreated to a dark cave in her mind where they could lie in wait. And she was happy to let them lie. For now, anyway.

Loth, for once, had had the presence of mind to call an ambulance as he'd hurtled down the stairs. He'd told Clara afterward that he'd had the urge to jump after Nate. They'd always followed each other everywhere. Once Nate had been taken to the hospital, Loth never left his side.

The coroner's report stated that Coppelius had died of a heart attack. Probably, they said, from the combination of being startled by the fireworks and the shock of having Nate jump from the tower directly in front of him. Clara had bowed her head, murmuring about what a shame it was. In the weeks that followed, they'd waited for someone to come forward and claim his body, but no one ever did, and eventually, the hospital cremated him and stored him in a small, non-descript box on a shelf, somewhere in its cavernous basement—but not before donating parts of him to science, including his eyes.

Once he'd recovered enough to speak, Nate demanded the surgeons remove the chips in his head—all of them.

"But Coppelius is gone, Nate. He's dead." She'd considered keeping how Coppelius had died a secret from Nate but decided against it. Their secrets had kept them apart for far too long.

At first, he'd been incredulous, putting down his lack of comprehension to the medication flowing through his veins. She'd had to explain it to him several times before he understood.

"You...you tricked Coppelius into believing you'd stabbed him with a sword? A *sword*? In the middle of Portfade? And he believed it so thoroughly he had a heart attack? I just...it doesn't make any sense. How did he not see through it?"

"Anything can seem real if the seed is already there, Nate," she reminded him gently. "You know that better than anyone. It's perfectly logical when you think about it."

But despite Coppelius being dead, he'd insisted.

It took Clara longer to relent. "They can't remove them without damaging your—"

"I don't care, Clara. I don't want to live in fear. It's the only way I can know for sure."

In the end, she'd given in, not that it had been her decision to make. And despite her fears, Nate had emerged unscathed. He continued to make dreamscapes, and his creations, based on pure emotion rather than visuals, increased the recovery rates of certain patients by over eighty percent.

She'd worried at first that he would feel trapped in the work he'd tried to get away from, or that he was doing it out of obligation to her. But instead, he thrived. In fact, Nate now seemed more at peace with himself than he'd ever been. "I don't mind being blind, Clara. Do you know why?"

"Why?"

"Because the very last thing I saw was you, telling me you loved me. Do you remember?"

"I remember." She'd tried to say it calmly, gently, as though their future was assured. Inside, her heart had pleaded with him, begged him, just this once, to be the old Nate, the Nate who suffered fear and doubt, who wouldn't have risked the surgery. It was selfish, but when it came to him, she was.

"It gave me the strength to get through it. Your face being the last thing I ever saw, Clara? It was a gift."

"But you nearly died, Nate. You—" She would never get over the fear of losing him, no matter how restored to himself he was.

"I'm free, Clara. I'm finally free of the shadow that's been over me for most of my life. I know it's difficult to understand."

It was *impossible* to understand. Clara could never have made the decision Nate had. But she didn't need to understand it. She could carry the burden of that fear for him for the rest of their lives, if it kept that shadow at bay.

Clara resisted the urge to pinch herself, as she had so many times in the last few months. She wasn't dreaming, not anymore. All her dreams had come true.

Clara's dress dragged over the wildflowers as they made their way to Olympia's cottage. Today was a special day—Clara's birthday—and they'd planned to spend it with Loth and their new friend.

As they entered the clearing, a group of women were just saying their goodbyes. They smiled at Clara as they passed her, one of them waving shyly and dipping her head. Olympia stood on the stoop, watching them go, her face lighting up when she saw Nate and Clara.

"You're right on time." She glanced over Clara's shoulder as though looking for someone, and her smile fell just a little.

"How are your sessions going?" Clara pressed Nate's shoulder, and he eased himself down onto the picnic blanket spread on the grass.

Olympia, still in limbo, had begun running sessions for women who, like her, had been through severely traumatic experiences. Many of them were comatose, medically induced, as they underwent therapy, traveling from their safe spaces into hers. It was a long, delicate process, but already the doctors were marveling at the results and making recommendations for the process to become a standard option for patients.

"Good, I think. It's incredible what some of the women have survived." Olympia shook her head.

"It's incredible what *you* survived." Clara smiled at her.

"What we *all* survived." Olympia gazed down at Nate.

There was a sudden commotion in the rose bushes at the edge of the clearing. With the sound of tearing fabric, ripping leaves, and a few curses, Loth tumbled out.

"Why the hell isn't there a path here?" he demanded, pulling petals from his hair as he reached them.

"There is, Loth. Right *there*." Clara pointed the way she and Nate had come. "How could you possibly miss it?"

"I was trying to gather these." From behind his back, he brandished a bouquet of wildflowers, a little worse for wear. "Here." He handed them to Olympia then, to Clara's surprise, blushed. Actually *blushed*. And what was more, so did Olympia, looking for all the world like any other young woman whose heart was stirred.

And just when I thought my mine couldn't get any fuller. Clara threw her arms around him and kissed his cheek. "I'm on to you," she whispered.

"What am I missing?" Nate tilted his head toward them. "I know it's something good."

"Just Loth being a gentleman."

"*What?* And I'm missing it? I knew there would be a reason to leave those damn chips in."

"Oh, quit your grumbling, Nate. You wouldn't believe it even if you did see it." Loth tugged down his blazer. "Right. Shall we get on with it? Ari's been on me to go over some figures with her."

Yes, what was the surprise? Loth wouldn't tell Clara this morning when he'd told her the time and place of her birthday surprise—probably the first time in his life he'd ever managed to keep a secret. "What—"

Nate was on one knee, his hands held out in front of him. In them, he cradled a tiny coral box.

"Clara, I was going to write you a poem, but I'm sure both you and Olympia have had enough of those for a lifetime. Besides, I know you don't need words to know how I feel about you, how I've always felt about you. You've seen the darkest moments of my soul, and even when I couldn't see my love for you, you could, and you refused to let me go. You are the love of my life, Clara, and I've dreamed of this day for a long time. In fact, there were times when I thought this day would only ever be a dream, and—"

She pressed her fingers to her lips. "Quit while you're ahead, my love. I feel the beginning of a sonnet coming on."

Nate grinned. "Thank you. You know how carried away I can get, *especially* when it's about my love for you."

"All right, Nate. Give it up. You're raising the bar a bit too high." Loth glanced at Olympia then laughed self-consciously. She hid her smile behind her hand. Clara's heart threatened to burst.

Nate opened the box and Clara held her breath.

It was this moment that would prove whether Nate was truly okay. He'd felt cursed for so long, it could easily have tainted every aspect of his life, everything he loved. If the ring in that box was anything other than platinum and ruby, Coppelius had had the last word.

The red stone glittered defiantly under the overhead sun, the slim platinum band embracing the weight of its fire. The only thing that had changed was the inscription etched around the inside of the band, pressing against her flesh as he slipped it over her finger.

For Clara, my dreaming life. That we never wake up.

ABOUT THE AUTHOR

A.W. Cross is a made of 100% star stuff. She writes romantic social science fiction and lives in the gorgeous wilds of Canada with her beloved family and a deep nostalgia for the 80s.

Other books by A.W. Cross:

FOXWEPT ARRAY

Rose, Awake: A Futuristic Romance Retelling of Sleeping Beauty (Foxwept Array Short Story)

Pine, Alive: A Futuristic Romance Retelling of Pinocchio (Foxwept Array #1)

Beauty, Unmasked: A Futuristic Romance Retelling of Beauty and The Beast (Foxwept Array #3)

Lissa, Beautiful: A Futuristic Romance Retelling of The Frog Princess (Foxwept Array #4)

THE ARTILECT WAR

The Seeds of Winter: Artilect War Book One

The Gardener of Man: Artilect War Book Two

The Harvest of Souls: Artilect War Book Three

The Artilect War Complete Series